BSC in the USA

**Other books by
Ann M. Martin**

Leo the Magnificat
Rachel Parker, Kindergarten Show-off
Eleven Kids, One Summer
Ma and Pa Dracula
Yours Turly, Shirley
Ten Kids, No Pets
Slam Book
Just a Summer Romance
Missing Since Monday
With You and Without You
Me and Katie (the Pest)
Stage Fright
Inside Out
Bummer Summer

THE KIDS IN MS. COLMAN'S CLASS series
BABY-SITTERS LITTLE SISTER series
THE BABY-SITTERS CLUB mysteries
THE BABY-SITTERS CLUB series

BSC in the USA

Ann M. Martin

An
APPLE
PAPERBACK

SCHOLASTIC INC.
New York Toronto London Auckland Sydney

Cover art by Hodges Soileau

Interior art by Angelo Tillery

No part of this publication may be reproduced in whole or in part, or stored in a retrieval system, or transmitted in any form or by any means, electronic, mechanical, photocopying, recording, or otherwise, without written permission of the publisher. For information regarding permission, write to Scholastic Inc., 555 Broadway, New York, NY 10012.

ISBN 0-590-69216-X

12 11 10 9 8 7 6 5 4 3 2   7 8 9/9 01 2/0

Printed in the U.S.A.   40

First Scholastic printing, July 1997

The author gratefully acknowledges
Peter Lerangis
for his help in
preparing this manuscript.

Special thanks to
Bonnie Bryant, Clifton Lewis,
Peter Rogers, and Janet Vultee

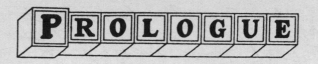

PROLOGUE

Tuesday

Dear Sunny,
  Guess what? I'll be seeing
you soon, back in good old
Palo City, CA.
  I know, I know. Jeff
and I were supposed to
spend the whole summer
in Stoneybrook, not just
half.
  But Dad just called from
Palo City. He canceled our
plane reservations. Instead,
we're going to leave a
couple of weeks early.
In an old, beat-up RV.

  Who's driving?
  Dad.
  How can he do that if he's
already in California?
  He's going to fly here first.
  With his RV tucked under
his airplane seat?

1

No. The RV belongs to
Mr. Choi, Dad's art dealer
friend from New York.
Mr. Choi is moving to
L.A., but he doesn't
have time to drive the
RV himself.

So Dad volunteered—
but only if Mr. Choi
would let him take
along Jeff and me.

Nothing like advance
notice, huh? When Dad
asked us, I thought:

WHY IS HE DOING
THIS? ARRGGHHH!

No way! Frankly, I
was just settling in
here. I even have some
baby-sitting assignments
with the BSC. Besides,
Jeff likes playing with
his cute little pals here,
and he loves the way
Mom fusses over him.

You think your so smart!
Comments courtesy
of my nosy, sneaky
brother.

Anyway, you know Dad. He can be very persuasive. First he convinced Jeff and me that the trip would be fun. Then he mentioned the idea to Mom. She, of course, nearly blew a gasket. But somehow Dad and she worked out a custody swap — so off we go!

One problem: RVs are absolutely horrible for the environment. Do you know anything about them? Can they run on low-emission ethanol? Let me know.

I'll keep you posted. More later.

Wednesday

I broke the news of the RV trip at the Baby-sitters Club meeting. I thought my friends would be freaked.

They're not. In fact, they want to follow us. In a blimp. Who's idea is this? Kristy Thomas's, of course.

Hmmm. I think I'll hold on to this letter until I see what happens....

Friday

My jaw is still scraping the ground.

Kristy's stepdad thinks a cross-country trip is a great idea. Not in a blimp, though. He wants to cancel his family's vacation plans, rent an RV of his own, and take all the Brewer/Thomases across country — along with any of Kristy's friends who can fit!

I thought Kristy would say no to the idea. She's so strict about Baby-

sitters Club meetings.
But she figures business
will be slow enough for
us to take off two weeks.

                    Saturday
    Dad is so competitive.
Now HE'S inviting my
friends to come along
with us. Which is a
good thing because
we couldn't all fit in
one RV anyway.
    Mary Anne, the
World's Most Loyal
Stepsister, asked her
dad, Richard, the
World's Most Cautious
Stepfather, if she
could go. He acted as
if she wanted to go to
Antarctica on a raft.
(Sigh.)
    More to follow. Check
your mailbox tomorrow.

The count: Stacey
McGill, yes. (She'll go
in our RV.)
Abby Stevenson, yes.
(In Kristy's.)
Claudia Kishi, possibly.
Mary Anne and I
are still working on
Richard.
Please please please
please...

I cannot believe it.
I am shocked. Flab-
bergasted. I am pinching
myself between sentences.
I will write this and then
check it again tomorrow
morning before I finally
mail this letter, just to
make sure it really hap-
pened.

Guess what? Richard
gave in. Mary Anne
can go!
So can Claudia.
Jessi Ramsey and
Mallory Pike are still

leaning on their parents.
   Could it be? Could
this be the first Baby-
sitters Club cross-
country road trip?
   I know it's going to
happen. I just know it.
   It's BSC ACROSS
AMERICA!
   Yyyyyyyyessssssss!
   I'll talk to you soon.

                    Luv,
                    Dawn

Dawn

Saturday

Well, diary, tomorrow is the big day. But I am already nervous today. I almost drank Richard's coffee. I thought it was my herbal tea. It's a good thing I smelled it in time. Otherwise I might be barfing until September. Yecchhhh!

Oh, well. Everybody was a little jittery at breakfast. Mainly because of Dad, I think. Seeing him in Stoney-brook is so weird. For all of us...

"Not bad," Dad said, eating his western omelette, "considering it was made on this side of the country."

"Mmmm," agreed Mary Anne.

"Thank you," said Richard.

"Needs salt," grumped Jeff.

Nothing, said Mom.

We all chewed. The stove clock clicked to 9:35.

Dad smiled and took another bite. "Yup. It's about as western as cactus."

"Daaaaad," I said.

Dad laughed. "I didn't mean tastewise!"

Mom put her napkin down. "Will you excuse me, please?"

Ugh.

Breakfast was not off to a good start.

I had been so excited about seeing my dad. This was his very first visit to Stoneybrook. When I saw the humongous old RV pull into our driveway that morning, I was practically screaming with joy.

Now, in the middle of breakfast, I felt horrible.

The chemistry was off. Way off. Dad's sense of humor wasn't working. The atmosphere in the kitchen was about as cheery as a hospital waiting room.

Dawn

Divorce sure does weird things to people.

Before that day, Richard and Dad had never met. Also, Mom and Dad have stayed on opposite ends of the country since their divorce. They have not even been in the same state together, let alone the same room. I can't tell you how many hours I've spent in an airplane shuttling between the two of them.

Where do *I* live? Palo City, California, with Dad. I used to live here, in Stoneybrook, Connecticut. This summer, I was just visiting.

Confusing? It's not. Just the simple story of Bicoastal Dawn.

You see, I was born and raised in Palo City. But after my parents split up, Mom decided to move with Jeff and me back to her hometown, which happens to be Stoneybrook. She wanted to be near her fond memories — and her parents, who still live here.

From the very start, Jeff couldn't make the adjustment. He was miserable. Eventually Mom let him move back with Dad. We were sad to see him go, but we knew he'd be happier. I was pretty homesick for California, too, but I had something Jeff didn't have. The Baby-sitters Club.

The BSC members are my absolute best East Coast friends. The club meets three times a week (Mondays, Wednesdays, and Fridays, from five-thirty until six) in Claudia Kishi's bedroom, to answer calls from local parents who need sitters. When I lived in Stoneybrook, I was the BSC's alternate officer. I took over the duties of the president, vice-president, secretary, or treasurer whenever any of them was absent.

If I hadn't joined the BSC, I might not have gained my stepfamily.

Soon after I arrived here, I became close to Mary Anne. She introduced me to the BSC. Meantime, we both discovered a deep, dark secret our parents shared. They had been in serious LUV in high school! But my grandparents had dashed their romance. They thought Richard wasn't good enough for their daughter, so they pressured Mom to break up with him and go away to college. It was bye-bye, Stoneybrook, and hello, heartbreak. (Sob, sob.)

Well, both of them recovered. Mom married Dad, of course, and had Jeff and me. Richard married, too, but Mrs. Spier died when Mary Anne was a baby. Richard was devastated. He became super-protective of Mary Anne and raised her very strictly, insisting she follow lots of rules. She had to wear little-girl clothes and pigtails right up until seventh grade.

By the time I met Mary Anne, Richard had loosened up a bit. (At least Mary Anne said so.

He still seemed stuffy to me.) When we found out their secret, *zoom* — Dawn and Mary Anne, Matchmakers Inc., sprang into action! And boy, did those old sparks fly. (Personally, I wouldn't have predicted it. Richard's a nice guy but super-organized and conservative; Mom is funny, absentminded, and full of life. Oh, well, I guess opposites attract.)

Anyway, Mary Anne and Richard moved into our house, this incredibly cool two-hundred-year-old farmhouse with a hidden passageway. Life was perfect.

Sort of.

Unfortunately, my homesickness really started kicking in. The more I visited Dad and Jeff, the more I knew I had to move back to California. Believe me, leaving Mary Anne and Mom was not easy, but we've dealt well with the separation.

Two lives, two coasts. Both fabulous. I always feel a little split, but I consider myself very lucky.

In Life One (Palo City), I have a new step-mom. Her name's Carol, and she's kind of a blabbermouth, but we get along okay. (She couldn't take our trip because of her job.) I also have a circle of fantastic friends. My absolute closest one is Sunny Winslow. We grew up together. She and I and two other girls (Jill Henderson and Maggie Blume) started our own baby-sitting organization, the We ❤ Kids Club. It's much more casual than the BSC — picture poolside meetings with a cell phone and a big spread of natural snacks. Yes, natural. We're all super-conscious about healthy eating and the environment.

As you can imagine, being bicoastal means my life is full of tearful farewells and reunions. But none had been quite as tense as this one.

Dad was eyeing Mom as she ran to the bathroom. "Was it something I said?" he asked.

Richard put his napkin on the table. "I'll check on her."

Off he went.

Munch, munch, chew, chew, sip, sip.

"So!" Dad blurted out. "Did everyone pick out a special place to visit on our little cross-country cruise?"

Gulp. Dad had asked us about this already. I'd planned to study a map of the U.S. and come up with a suggestion, but had I done that? Noooo.

"Hawaii!" Jeff blurted out.

"Uh, stick to the mainland, please," Dad said.

"I want to repel!" Jeff announced.

"You do repel already," I remarked.

Jeff stuck out his tongue. "It's a rock-climbing word."

"*Rappel*," Dad said. "Maybe a lesson in some national park out West?"

"All riiiight!" Jeff whooped.

Where to go. . . . My mind was racing.

I thought about a book I'd been reading. A ghost story about an abandoned gold-mining town out West.

"A ghost town!" I blurted out. "That's where I want to go."

"*Whaaat?*" Jeff said. "That's dumb. How are we going to find one?"

"Look for a ghost and follow it," said Dad with a straight face. "Mary Anne?"

Mary Anne was pushing her omelette around her plate, deep in thought. "I'm not sure yet, either. Sorry."

"Don't make it someplace like a fabric store," Jeff murmured.

"Jeff, that did it!" I picked up a bagel and aimed.

"Yikes!" Jeff was off like a shot. He nearly collided with Mom and Richard, who were walking back toward the kitchen.

"Duck!" Jeff yelled.

"Unidentified flying bagel!" Dad exclaimed.

Whirrrrr — splat! The aliens crash-landed in a panful of soapy water in the sink.

Richard snorted a laugh.

Mary Anne cracked up. So did Jeff.

The poor little bagel was floating in the suds like a shrunken inner tube.

I could see Mom's shoulders loosening up. She shook her head and started to chuckle.

Suddenly I relaxed. Mom would survive just fine.

I was feeling better and better about our trip. What an adventure! Finally I'd be crossing the USA on the road and seeing some of those places I always fly over.

Too bad I'd never looked for ghosts through my jumbo-jet windows.

But I was determined to find some.

Kristy

OFFICIAL BABY-SITTERS CLUB
CROSS-USA TRIP JOURNAL
BREWER DIVISION

Sunday

Well, it's opening day of the BSC cross-country marathon, folks. At the moment, we're riding in a team van with the Brewer family and Abby Stevenson. Any quotes from the dugout for this, our official trip journal?

ELVIS, here I come!!!!!!!

Graceland. Former home of the King of Rock and Roll. Just one of the many stops on the Grand Tour.

We're now pulling up to Kishi Central, where the rest of the players have gathered. I can see the Schafer team already loading up. Here we will divvy up before the trip.

If you're keeping tabs, the Brewer brigade is swinging south; the Schafer shift, north. Both will end up in Palo City! And heeeeere are the tentative lineup cards:

BREWER RV
Watson Brewer
Elizabeth Thomas Brewer
Karen Brewer
Andrew Brewer
David Michael Thomas
Abigail Stevenson
Jessica Ramsey
Mallory Pike
Kristy Thomas

SCHAFER RV
Jack Schafer
Dawn Schafer
Jeff Schafer
Mary Anne Spier
Claudia Kishi
Stacey McGill

"Love meeee tenderrrrr . . ." warbled Abby Stevenson in her best Elvis Presley imitation. "Pack theese baaags . . ."

"Oww-oww-owwwwww!" howled David Michael Thomas.

"Don't be rude," scolded Karen Brewer.

Abby took David Michael in her arms and began dancing him around the RV. "Neverrr let me go-o-o-o . . ." she sang.

"EWWWWWWWW!" David Michael shot away as if Abby were covered with lice.

David Michael is my little brother. Karen is my stepsister. They're both seven. I also have two older brothers, Charlie Thomas (who's seventeen) and Sam Thomas (fifteen), a four-year-old stepbrother named Andrew Brewer, and a two-and-a-half-year-old adopted sister named Emily Michelle Thomas Brewer. My family is B&B. Big and blended. We live in a mansion in Stoneybrook.

My stepfather, Watson Brewer, is a millionaire. He works at home as a consultant, and he can take time off whenever he wants. Those are three reasons why he was able to rent the RV for this trip.

I was so happy he did. Too bad my whole family couldn't go. Sam and Charlie were at camp. Emily Michelle was staying home with my grandmother, Nannie, who lives with us.

Now, at the curb in front of Claudia's house, Watson and Mom were loading suitcases into the RV cargo hold. All my other BSC friends were milling around, jabbering away.

"We're already running out of room," Watson remarked.

"Oh?" said Mr. Schafer. "I was hoping you'd take some of Claudia's luggage."

Claudia was standing with her family near Mr. Schafer's RV, looking sheepish. Around her were three bulging suitcases the size of small hippos.

"We warned you, Claudia," said her sister, Janine.

"I could leave behind a down jacket," Claudia suggested.

"You brought a *down jacket*?" Abby asked.

"Two," Claudia said, "because you never know how cold it'll be. We *are* going north. Anyway, one is my Eddie Bauer basic red, for casual cold, but the other is more a dinner-out, full-length one, just in case. . . ."

Mr. and Mrs. Kishi were already rolling the suitcases back toward the house.

Jessi Ramsey, out of pure excitement, was doing ballet leaps around the RV. Mallory Pike was digging into her luggage, looking for something. Stacey McGill was combing her hair in the side mirror. Mary Anne and her boyfriend, Logan, were holding hands and being all gooey-eyed with each other. David Michael was giggling and making kissy noises.

I was glad it wasn't too early. The neighbors would have been throwing things at us.

"I'm thirsty!" cried Andrew from inside our vehicle.

"But you just drank apple juice," retorted Mom.

"Anybody see my *Misty* book?" Mallory called out. "I put it down on top of my suitcase."

"Check the floor of the car!" Stacey shouted.

"It's not a car," Jeff corrected her. "It's an RV."

"What does RV stand for, anyway?" Mary Anne asked.

"Ridiculous Vehicle," Watson said, looking up at the two enormous wheeled monsters parked at Claudia's curb.

"When are we going to leave?" demanded Jeff.

"I'm still thirsty!" Andrew screamed.

Utter, total chaos. A person could hardly hear herself think.

I tried to tune them out. No goofing around for me. We hadn't finished our planning, and *somebody* had to concentrate on it. Three-thousand-plus miles, two RVs, fifteen people with fifteen different destinations — it was an organizational nightmare.

I was holding a clipboard, staring at the trip lineup. Something was not right.

"We're unbalanced," I said.

Mr. Schafer looked forlornly at the cargo hold. "I know."

"Not *suitcase* unbalanced," I continued, "*people* unbalanced. Nine in our RV, but only six in yours."

Watson's ears perked up. "This RV fits only seven comfortably, eight in a pinch."

"Can we switch somebody?" Mr. Schafer asked.

"We divided up the norths and souths," I said. "But there are some undecideds."

"Mr. Schafer, how about two suitcases and a backpack?" Claudia shouted from her front door.

"Andrew spilled his apple juice!" cried Karen from inside the RV.

Zoom. Off went the two dads to do damage control.

Time to switch into problem mode.

I, Kristy Thomas, am a problem specialist. When other people shrink away, I hop into action.

If you think I'm exaggerating, ask any of the girls crowding into the RVs. We all belong to the Baby-sitters Club. Who invented the Baby-sitters Club? Me.

The BSC was a solution to a problem.

One day, back before Mom met Watson, she was trying to find a sitter for David Michael. I couldn't baby-sit that evening, and neither could Charlie or Sam. My dad was out of the picture. He had run away from my family soon after David Michael was born. (That's right, run away. How many times has he visited? Once. And I hear from him once or twice a year if I'm lucky. The postmark of his last letter was from a place called Sausalito, wherever that is.) Anyway, poor Mom phoned all over town and couldn't line up a single sitter.

The concept hit me: a regular group of sitters, using a central phone number. Simple, right? It had Duh written all over it. (Most Great Ideas do.) *Zing*. The BSC was born. We decided to use Claudia's room as headquarters because she has a private phone line. We started with four members, but now we have ten — seven regulars; two associates, who help us out when we're overloaded; and one honorary member (Dawn, who lives in California).

Needless to say, tons of Stoneybrook parents have become our clients, and they love us.

We're all great with kids, we're super-reliable and friendly, we're prompt, and we often bring Kid-Kits to our jobs. Kid-Kits are boxes of old toys, puzzles, books, and odds and ends. (Pretty basic stuff, but kids adore them.)

Success does have its own problems. We're usually so busy that we can't guarantee the same sitter for the same family each time. Kristy the problem specialist to the rescue! I set up something called the BSC notebook. In it, we write a description of each job, including any new information the next sitter might need to know — house rules, bedtimes, fears, habits, and so on.

We're really more like a tightly knit, well-managed company than a club. We collect dues. We have rules and officers. I am president, which means I run the meetings. I also dream up new ideas, not only for club publicity but for the enjoyment of our clients' kids (we call them our charges).

Claudia's our vice-president, mainly because she hosts meetings. She's also a junk food maniac, which means our meetings are major pig-outs. Her parents are super-strict about nutrition, but Claudia has lots of junk food hiding places, especially among her art supplies. Claudia loves to draw, paint, sculpt, and make jewelry. She dresses artistically, too — her outfits are put together from funky stuff she buys in thrift shops. She's also, in my opinion, drop-dead stunning, with jet black hair and dark, almond-shaped eyes (she's Japanese-American).

Claudia is nothing like the rest of the Kishi family. They all dress in the world's most conservative clothes and have zero interest in art. Mr. Kishi's a high-powered investment banker, Mrs. Kishi's a librarian, and Janine's a genius high school student who takes college courses. Claudia, on the other hand, cannot write a sentence without a spelling error. Her grades were so low she was sent back to seventh grade (Mary Anne, Stacey, Abby, Dawn, and I are in eighth). Fortunately, she's doing just fine now.

Mary Anne, my best friend in the world, is the BSC secretary. She's in charge of the record book, which contains our official calendar. When a client calls with a job request, Mary Anne knows at a glance who's available. She records every single job plus all our conflicts: doctor appointments, family trips, and after-school activities. In the back of the book she keeps a client list that includes names, addresses, rates paid, and basic information about our charges.

Mary Anne, as you can imagine, is extremely

organized. Also sweet and shy. She's the world's most sensitive listener, and she cries at the slightest sad thing.

Mary Anne and I grew up next door to each other. Kids used to think we were related. Even now we look somewhat alike — we're both about five feet tall, with dark brown eyes and hair. But Mary Anne has short hair and kind of a preppy wardrobe. (Me? Ponytail, jeans, T-shirts all the way.)

Stacey says I have fashion-blindness. She tracks clothing trends the way Watson tracks the stock market. (Personally, both things make me snoozy.) One of her favorite clothing colors is black. According to her, it sets off her blonde hair. Besides, she was born and raised in New York City, and she says native New Yorkers wear black all year long. Uh-huh. Maybe they change whenever I visit, because I always notice *lots* of different-colored outfits. (I love going to NYC. Stacey's divorced dad lives there. At least *her* father keeps in touch. Hrrmmmph.)

As BSC treasurer, Stacey collects weekly dues and pays monthly expenses: Claudia's phone bill, gas money for my private chauffeur (my brother Charlie, who drives Abby and me to meetings), and supplies for Kid-Kits. Stacey keeps close track of the treasury. She's a real math whiz. Her favorite occasion is a surplus . . . then it's pizza party time!

Pizza is one of the few kinds of junk food Stacey can eat. She has diabetes. That means her body cannot process sugars well. If she eats candy she could become ill, even go into a coma. As long as Stacey watches her diet very, very carefully, has meals at regular intervals, and gives herself daily injections of insulin, she can lead a normal life. (I know, the injection part sounds gross, but Stacey insists it's about as painful as brushing her teeth.)

What happens, you may ask, if one of our officers is sick? The alternate officer takes charge. That was Dawn's job before she moved. Dawn (who, by the way, has long, light blonde hair, blue eyes, and freckles) is a real individualist. If you want to hear strong opinions, start her talking about the environment or nutrition.

We missed Dawn after she moved — as a friend and as a baby-sitter. We tried to survive shorthanded, but it didn't work. We were swamped. Too swamped even to look for a new member. I thought I was going to go nuts.

And then . . . ta-da! Abby Stevenson landed in our laps. Well, not literally. She, her twin sister, Anna, and their mom moved into a house on my block. (Abby's dad died in a car crash when she was nine.)

I liked Abby and Anna right away. *Wild* is the best word to describe Abby — wild sense of humor, wild hair. It flows around her head in big ringlets (the hair, not the humor). Unlike most of my friends, Abby's a good athlete (yeeeaa!), despite asthma problems and tons of allergies. Anna's much different — quieter and gentler, like Mary Anne. She's also a phenomenal violinist who practices four hours a day. And she hates sports.

Sometimes it's hard to believe they're twins. Sometimes it's not. Take their Bat Mitzvah, for instance. That's a ritual many Jewish girls go through at age thirteen. You have to recite in Hebrew from the Torah, the holy book of Judaism. All the BSC members were invited to the twins' ceremony. On that day, you knew Abby and Anna were twins. They were equally wonderful.

We invited both girls to join the BSC. Anna said no, mainly because of her music studies. But Abby took Dawn's place as alternate officer, and she's fit in beautifully.

So far, all the members I've mentioned are thirteen. Our two junior officers, Jessi and Mallory, are eleven and in sixth grade. They're best friends. They also happen to be the oldest kids in their families, and they both insist their parents treat them like babies. Both of them were convinced they wouldn't be allowed to go on this trip (boy, were they surprised when their parents said yes). Two other things they have in common: They're fantastic with kids, and they love to read, especially horse books.

In some ways Jessi and Mallory are very different. Jessi's African-American, and she lives and breathes ballet. She wears her hair in a tight bun and carries herself with perfect posture. She has one younger sister and a baby brother. Mal's white, with thick, floppy reddish-brown hair. She wears glasses and braces and walks like an average person. Her great passion is writing and illustrating her own stories, and she has *seven* younger siblings.

Our two associates, who help us out when we're totally overloaded, are Logan Bruno and Shannon Kilbourne. Both are in eighth grade. Logan is Mary Anne's steady boyfriend. He's pretty cute, I guess — dimply and sandy-haired, with a faint Southern accent. He plays after-school sports, so his baby-sitting time is limited. Shannon goes to a private school called Stoneybrook Day School, and she's involved in all kinds of extracurricular activities there.

Neither of them could go on this trip. Shannon's at sleepaway camp. Logan is working as a busboy at a local restaurant and playing in a summer baseball league. (Which explains why Mary Anne was now blubbering away.)

Amid the blubberings and screamings and laughings, I, Kristy, was tackling the Dilemma of the Uneven RVs.

First I needed to figure out who could switch. Just about everyone had picked a destination. Who needed to go where? Time for some geography.

I started writing:

BREWER

me: As many major-league ballparks as possible

(I wanted to do this with my dad when I was a kid, but you know what happened. I figured I might as well do it myself.)

mallory: Chinkateeg

(If you're not a horse book fan, that's some island in Virginia where wild ponies run around. If you *are* a fan, don't laugh at my spelling. I know it's wrong.)

mom: still undecided; "something scenic"

andrew: San Diego Zoo

Kristy

(By the time we arrive, a panda may be giving birth.)

Abby: Graceland, the former home of Elvis Presley

(Abby worships Elvis.)

David Michael: A rodeo, anywhere

Jessi: Dalton, Mississippi

(Jessi's ancestors were slaves on a plantation there. She wants to find out all she can about them.)

Karen: Four Corners

(It's a place out West where four states touch. Karen wants to experience being in all of them at the same time.)

Watson: Lester, Oklahoma

(Some of his college friends live there. Why anyone would live in a place called Lester, I don't know.)

SCHAFER:
Stacey: Seattle

(She's been writing to a guy she knows named Ethan, who is spending the summer there with his parents.)

Dawn: A ghost town, anywhere

MaryAnne: Maynard, Iowa

(That's where her grandmother lives.)

Claudia: The Art Institute of Chicago

(Knowing Claud, she probably had a hard time choosing between this and Hershey Park.)

Mr. Schafer: San Francisco

(He insists it's the coolest city in the USA. Maybe he hasn't been to New York.)

Jeff: Yellowstone National Park

(Rock climbing.)

I put a big star next to the travelers in our RV who could possibly go north.

Watson peered over my shoulder. "Figured it out?"

"Mom, David Michael, or I have to move," I said.

Now Karen, Abby, Dawn, David Michael, and Mr. Schafer were crowding around. Karen looked very concerned. "We have to split up the family?"

"I could go in the other RV," Abby volunteered, "if Mr. Schafer can swing down to Memphis."

Mr. Schafer shook his head. "Then north to Chicago afterward? That's really out of the way."

"Come with us, David Michael," Dawn suggested. "You can find a rodeo in a northern state like Montana."

"I want to go with Mom!" David Michael said.

Mom was stepping out of the RV. "You will, darling. The Grand Canyon is south, too. We'll have to stay in this van."

Abby suddenly sneezed. "Did you say Grad Cadyod?" (Abby's allergies were kicking in.) "Is that your choice?"

"Yes," Mom replied. "Have you been there?"

"Isd't it very crowded this tibe of year? Hot, too. Add overrud with gray wolves add stuff."

"Well, I hadn't thought of that," Mom said, looking a little bewildered.

"Gray wolves have every bit as much right to the land as humans do," Dawn proclaimed.

"Modumet Valley is supposed to be a huddred tibes better!" Abby pressed on. "Add it's south, too!"

"Maybe we can stop on the way," Watson suggested.

I looked closely at the list and sighed. The solution was clear. "I guess I'll have to switch."

"Just a moment!" Watson protested.

"This was supposed to be a family vacation," Mom said.

"I cud thik of a dortherd place for byself," Abby volunteered.

"Nope, I insist," I said. "Really. I *want* to do it this way. We'll all be together in California and on the way home."

"But what about your ballparks?" Karen asked.

"Well, if I went south I couldn't see a lot of the best ones," I replied, "like Wrigley Field."

"Is that where they grow the gum trees or something?" David Michael asked.

Karen burst out laughing. "That is so silly."

"No sillier than going to see the home of Elvis Pretzel," David Michael retorted.

"Heyyyy, watch it," Abby said.

"Well," Mom said with a sigh. "We'll miss you —"

"Hooray! I did it!" Claudia's voice called from her front door. "Only two suitcases!"

Mr. Schafer forced a smile. "Well, that's good news."

Kristy

"Uh, don't forget," I said, "now you have to add mine."

Mr. Schafer went pale. He rolled up his sleeves and slumped toward the cargo hold.

We had a long, long way to go.

CHAPTER 3

Jessi

Entering Oakley, New Jersey — Sunday

We're back in my hometown — yeaaaa! I'm all fluttery inside. It feels as if my Big Mac and fries are doing a pas de deux up and down the walls of my stomach.

Weird. I have never felt this way during any

of my other visits. I guess that's because I've always been with my family. This is the first time my friends will see Oakley.

Okay, Ramsey. Calm down. We're all going to have a great time. Home cooking. Lots of laughs. Right?

Okra.

Fried chicken.

Biscuits with lots of butter.

How many times had I smelled those things as I walked up Grandma's front stoop? A hundred? A thousand?

It didn't matter. I still practically had to suck down my saliva.

I bounded up the walkway ahead of Watson, Mrs. Brewer, Andrew, Karen, Mallory, Abby, and David Michael.

I pressed the bell and knocked at the same time. (You have to do both, in case Grandpa's not home. Grandma's hearing is not so great.)

"Cute house," Watson remarked, looking around.

"Old, huh?" I said with a laugh. My grandparents' house is exactly like them — a little worn and faded, but sturdy and warm and inviting.

I felt a tingle as I wiped my feet on the familiar old mat that read, OUR HOUSE IS YOUR HOUSE. "Grandma hasn't changed the interior one bit since she moved here," I explained. "My dad's room is exactly the way it was when he went to college —"

Abby perked up. "Does he have any Elvis memorabilia?"

"He's not *that* old!" Mal exclaimed.

"Ahem," Watson said, arching his eyebrow. "I happen to have been something of a fan myself."

Mal's face turned red. "Oops."

"Well, Daddy was more of a Motown kind of guy, anyway," I said. "He says Elvis stole from a lot of the black singers in the fifties."

"Stole?" Abby looked skeptical.

"You know, sang their songs, imitated the way they sang and moved . . ." I rang and knocked again. Then I leaned close to the open window. "Grandma? Grandpa?"

A car puttered to a stop behind us, and a deep voice called out, "What are you standing around for? The door's open!"

"Grandpa!" I ran down the front steps and threw my arms around him as he climbed out of his old Buick.

His eyes were dancing. "Hello, baby!" he said. "Early, aren't you?"

Uh-oh. His voice sounded a little muffled. "Grandpa," I whispered, "you didn't forget to put in your —?"

"Choppers? Shush, child, you're beginning to sound like your grandmother!"

I couldn't help giggling. All my life, Grandma has always been bugging him to wear his false teeth — and all my life, Grandpa has never listened.

"We-e-e-ell, look who's here!" my grand-mother's voice sang out from the house. "Come in! I know this one, don't I?"

Grandma was standing in the open door now, her hand resting on Mallory's shoulder. "I'm Mallory Pike," Mal said meekly. "Remember Jessi's ballet? We met there?"

Before Grandma could reply, I was up the stoop and wrapping my arms around her. "Hi!" I squealed.

I introduced everyone all around. Grandpa nodded with a closemouthed smile, while Grandma gave him her sternest *I've-told-you-time-and-time-again-Arthur-Ramsey* Look.

As we walked into the living room, Grandpa scurried to fetch his teeth. Grandma settled into her big easy chair by the fireplace, and everyone sat on the old, comfortable couches and chairs. I pulled out the bench from Grandma's upright piano for Mallory and me.

"Well!" Grandma said with a sigh. "I am so glad I started that chicken early. I hope you all are hungry."

"Starving!" David Michael blurted out.

Grandma was up in a flash. "Would you like a little something now?"

Watson and Mrs. Brewer began fussing over David Michael — he didn't need the snack, he would ruin his appetite, typical grown-up stuff.

Jessi

But I was paying more attention to Mallory. She looked kind of stiff and uneasy. "Carsick?" I whispered.

Mal shook her head. "Nope. Fine."

"Are you sure?"

"Uh-huh."

I didn't believe her for a minute. I know Mal, and something was bothering her.

The smell? Couldn't be. Everybody loves fried chicken. Something in the living room? I gazed around at the familiar scene. Above the fireplace was a big color portrait photograph of my grandparents, my dad, my uncles John and Arthur, Jr., and my aunt Cecelia. It had been taken around the time my dad was in high school, and he and my uncles had these big Afros and wide-lapeled jackets. On the mantelpiece below the photo was Grandpa's collection of African statuettes.

I felt a sudden twist in my stomach.

I thought of the statuettes we have in our house. And of a girl named Alison I invited over one day, back when we first moved to Stoneybrook. Alison was white. She laughed hysterically at the statuettes. I didn't think much about that at first. Then she really started acting weird — like not accepting food that I had touched. When her parents came to pick her up, they were cold and uncomfortable. Her dad ac-

42

tually asked if more of "you people" were moving into town. (Needless to say, I did *not* stay
friends with Alison.) Mama and I talked about
the racism that Alison's family had shown.
Mama said, "Some people are afraid of the unknown."

Why did that pop into my mind? The look in
Mallory's eyes. The unease. It reminded me of
Alison.

Never, I said to myself.

Mallory could never be like that. She was a totally different kind of person. So were her parents. It was an insult to put Mallory and Alison
in the same thought.

But still . . .

Even in Oakley, racially mixed Oakley, kids
you never expected to do so would say racist
things when they were angry or stressed.

I tried to see this visit through Mallory's eyes.
I thought about Grandma's and Grandpa's
street, Wagner Lane. Tons of kids were playing
on it, all of them African-American. In Stoneybrook, my family lives on a quiet block, where
we're the *only* nonwhites. Then I thought about
the interior decoration of Grandpa's and
Grandma's house. It has a definite African
theme, much more so than our house.

Could it be? Were those things making Mallory uncomfortable?

Jessi

Was there a side of her I didn't know?

Ding-dong!

Before anyone could turn around, the front door opened and my cousin Keisha flew into the room. "Hiiiiii!"

All my ugly thoughts floated away. I screamed with joy. Behind Keisha were all the other Oakley Ramseys: Uncle John, Aunt Yvonne, and cousins Billy and Kara (Keisha's family); and Uncle Arthur, Aunt Denise, and their kids, Isaac and Raun.

The room exploded with noise. I hugged so many times, my arms grew tired. I tried to introduce everyone, but it was useless. Within about five minutes, my uncles were laughing at the top of their lungs with Watson, Aunt Yvonne was yakking with Mrs. Brewer, Aunt Denise was hugging Abby, Keisha was hugging Grandma, and Grandpa was back in the room, smiling brightly with his shiny false teeth.

I love my family. They are so loud and funny and affectionate.

As Keisha and I gabbed away, catching up, I caught a glimpse of Mallory. She was standing by the wall near the piano, alone.

Keisha followed my glance. She did a double take, then put her fists on her hips and called out, "Girl, what are you doing in that corner?"

Mallory practically jumped. "Oh . . . hi!"

Keisha bounded across the room and wrapped her in a big hug.

"Jessica, dear, would you please help me with the food?" I heard Grandma ask.

"Sure." I turned away and followed her into the kitchen. The smells didn't seem quite so luscious anymore. I began worrying about the okra. Would Mallory hate it? I tried to remember if Mama and Daddy had ever served it to her before.

"Nice people," Grandma said. "Got to shake out that Mallory, though. She's wound up tighter than a cobra."

"You noticed, too?" I asked.

Grandma lifted the lid off the okra pot and stirred. "Mmmm, this'll cure her."

Gulp.

I had to tell her what was on my mind. "Grandma —"

"So, where are you all headed after this?" Grandma barreled on.

"Well, first to Chincoteague, to see wild ponies, and then Dalton, Mississippi —"

Grandma dropped the wooden spoon into the okra, then quickly picked it up. "Why ever are you going to *Dalton*?"

"Well, that's where our ancestors were slaves, right? That's what you always told me. I want to see if I can learn more about them.

Jessi

There's an exhibit at the plantation. Photos and records."

Now Grandma was facing me. Her face had changed. At first I thought she was angry. But that wasn't it. She was looking at me the way I see her look at Daddy sometimes. Firm. Respectful. Like a grown-up to a grown-up. I felt a little shiver.

"Darling, I can't believe you decided to spend your vacation doing that." Grandma clucked her tongue and smiled. "At all of ten years old."

"Eleven," I reminded her. "Do you think I shouldn't?"

Grandma didn't answer for awhile. She began stirring the okra again. "I think you should," she finally said. "But be prepared, sweetheart."

"For what?" I asked. "I mean, I know it was harsh and awful and all . . ."

"What happened between the races was like an infection, Jessica. A virus. Back when our family was in Dalton, that virus was full-blown. What you see in those photos might not be too pretty." Grandma sighed. "Some people think the civil rights movement cured the sickness. But it didn't. Oh, sure, it made things better. But it was more like a vaccine. The infection is still inside people. Even the ones who think they're immune. Me and you."

And Mallory. The thought popped into my brain. I looked back toward the living room. Mallory was in full view now. She was laughing. Keisha was on one side of her, Isaac on the other. Little Kara, who's only two, was hugging Mal's legs.

Grandma saw it, too. She chuckled. "Looks like she finally got over the jitters, didn't she?"

"Well, some people are just afraid of the unknown, I guess," I said.

"Beg pardon?" Grandma gave me a puzzled look.

"Well, you know, she's not used to the . . . decor and the neighborhood —"

"She's your best friend, darling. The poor thing was worried about making a good impression, that's all."

Mallory saw me now and gave a cheerful wave. I waved back.

Wow.

Grandma's words hit me like a hammer.

She was right about Mallory, I just knew it.

I felt awful. Totally ashamed. Why hadn't I realized what was going on? Why had I assumed the worst?

I quietly began taking out silverware to set the table. I tried to piece together the thoughts tumbling in my mind.

I decided Grandma was right about another

Jessi

thing. Racism *is* like a disease. Even if you don't have it, it's still around in the air. And sometimes it affects the way you see things.

Whether you want it to or not.

Right about then, I started to feel nervous about what I'd find in Dalton. . . .

CHAPTER 4

Stacey

Monday

Dear Ethan,

Hi!! We are now entering Cleveland, Ohio. Have you ever been to Ohio? Let me tell you what it's like.

Flat.

I fell asleep in the RV and woke up twenty minutes later — and the view out the window was EXACTLY the same. I was sure we'd stalled. Nope. Mr. Schafer said he'd been driving the whole time.

My friend Kristy says I sound like a typical New Yorker. Ha. Personally, I think New Yorkers are very nice.

Well, maybe just some.

Me, at least. And you.

Anyway, I can't WAIT to see you!!!!! This feels like such an ADVENTURE, writing to you from the road!

Well, gotta go. We have to visit a baseball stadium. Kristy needs to buy a cap. She wants one from every stadium on our route. Zzzzzzz. (I suggested she buy them all back home. She stuck her tongue out at me.)

I hope you're not a big baseball fan. If you are, don't be mad! You're still meeting me at the CORNER COFFEE SHOP at NOON a WEEK FROM THURSDAY, right?

So far, we're keeping to our schedule. If anything changes, I'll write or call. Don't worry.

'Bye! See you soon!

Stacey

"The last Indian to win the Cy Young Award for pitching,'" read Kristy from a pamphlet, "'was Gaylord Perry, in 1972.'"

"Gaylord Perry doesn't sound like an Indian name," I remarked.

Kristy rolled her eyes. "*Cleveland* Indian."

"I knew that," I lied.

As we walked closer to Jacobs Field, a huge cheer rang out.

"Touchdown! The crowd goes wild!" Claudia called out.

Jeff groaned. "There are no *touchdowns* in baseball."

I gave Claudia a Look. So did Mary Anne and Dawn. We all cracked up.

Claudia's my best friend. She and Mary Anne may be the only people in the world who care less about baseball than I do.

Kristy insists it's a fun sport. Maybe she means *playing* it. But sitting around in the hot sun and watching grown men in ugly jumpsuits chase a little white ball? Not my idea of a good time.

Now, *basketball* I don't mind. It's faster, for one thing. And the players look great in those shorts.

Okay, maybe I'm still a little biased. I used to go out with a guy named Robert Brewster, who was on the Stoneybrook Middle School basketball team. In fact, he was my boyfriend when I met Ethan Carroll.

Nowadays I don't think much about basketball. (No, Ethan didn't break us up. Robert and I were already on the rocks.)

My mom says Ethan and I have an epistolary romance. I thought that had something to do with guns. But she explained it means a romance carried on through letters.

I don't know if I'd use the word *romance*. Yet.

Ethan and I have met only once, in New York City. He lives there. He's fifteen and absolutely, totally gorgeous — almost-black hair, blue eyes, broad shoulders, and cheekbones for days. Talented, too. His big goal in life is to become an artist. In fact, for the month of July, he was touring West Coast art galleries with his parents. (Mr. and Mrs. Carroll must be pretty cool, too.)

Which is why I was going to meet him in Seattle at the Corner Coffee Shop. Why that particular spot? Ethan is staying nearby, in his relatives' apartment. Besides, we New Yorkers love coffee shops. ("Coffee shop" is New Yorkese for "diner." Don't ask me why.)

Since we'd met, Ethan and I had been calling and writing. Mostly writing. I couldn't wait to see him in person again.

I was scared, too, to be honest. I mean, we

were still newlymets. What if I'd been wrong about him? What if he had some secret terrible quality, like picking his nose in public or a passion for baseball?

I guess I'd just have to take my chances.

"Get your Indians souvenirs here!" shouted a potbellied guy from a stand near the ballpark.

Kristy was already making a beeline.

W H O N N K - W H O N N K - W H O N N K - WHONNK! whonked an organ from inside the ballpark.

"Can't we go in?" Jeff asked his dad excitedly. "Please please please please?"

Puh-leeze.

"You can't just walk in, right in the middle of the game!" I exclaimed.

Mr. Schafer laughed. "Sure you can."

"Maybe I'm thinking of the theater," I murmured.

Kristy was walking back toward us, an Indians cap on her head and a huge smile on her face. "Got one!"

"We're going to the game!" Jeff announced.

"*Whaat?*" Claudia, Mary Anne, Dawn, and I said together.

"Yyyyyesss!" Kristy sprinted toward the ticket booth.

"But — but —" I sputtered.

"It's four against three, Dad," Dawn jumped in.

Then Mr. Schafer said the words I dreaded to hear. "I think it would be fun."

Off we trudged. Like prisoners to the dungeon.

What was the game like? Well, we stood up and cheered one home run, but we booed another. We participated in two waves. We ate hot dogs that tasted as if they'd been cooking since February. A foul ball whizzed into the stands nearby. Afterward, Claudia ducked each time she heard the crack of a bat. I managed to read an entire Cleveland travel guide, ads included, by the time the game ended.

That, as it turned out, saved the whole day. I showed Mr. Schafer the travel guide, and he went nuts over one particular place.

We were going to have our first official side trip . . .

P.S. News flash — the Cleveland Indians lost to the Boston some-things, 7-4. Too bad, huh?

Second news flash. Banner headline. Guess where we are headed now?

THE ROCK AND ROLL HALL OF FAME AND MUSEUM !!!

I LO-O-O-OVE Cleveland! More to follow.

XXXXXOOOOO,
Me

CHAPTER 5

Mallory ☺

I have been waiting for this day my
whole life. Well, at least *Tuesday* since I became
a Marguerite Henry fan. Which seems
like my whole life.

*Today we are
going to Chincoteague
Island. Home of
the wild ponies
and Pony Penning
Day. And Misty
and Stormy and
Sea Star and
Phantom and Paul
and Maureen Beebe.*

Easy, Jessi. You'll tear the page.
*I don't care, Mallory!
I'm still excited!!*

ME, TOO !!!!

Mallory

"I want to go to the ice-cream shop!" Andrew cried out.

"Me, too!" Abby exclaimed.

"Maybe it won't be so boring, after all," David Michael murmured.

"Seeing wild ponies on the beach is not boring!" Jessi remarked.

"Where are they?" Karen asked.

David Michael made a face. "There are no ponies here. No beach, either."

I was looking out the RV window. We were driving along Main Street of Chincoteague Island. Slowly. Traffic was bumper-to-bumper. I saw souvenir shops, restaurants, clothing stores, motels, boating supply stores, and jewelry shops. Tourists crowded the sidewalks. A storefront advertised a display of the original Misty, preserved.

"Misty is *stuffed*?" Jessi murmured.

The idea made me sick.

"Well . . . this is a nice place," Watson remarked.

"Quaint," Mrs. Brewer added.

Honk! Honk! blared a bus in front of us, spewing exhaust.

This wasn't at all what I was expecting. This wasn't the Chincoteague Island I'd read about. Chincoteague was a little village where kids ran around barefoot in the streets and old folks swapped stories on the front porch. At least it was in all the Marguerite Henry books.

Have you read them? You should, even if you're not a horse fan like me. The stories are great — especially the legend of the wild ponies.

You see, back in the 1500s, a cargo of stallions escaped from a shipwrecked Spanish galleon, swam to a nearby island, and made it their home. You can still see their descendants today, running wild and free. (Historians say there's no proof of this, but I believe it.)

The ponies are actually on nearby Assateague Island, which is almost forty miles long. Chincoteague is tucked snugly between it and the mainland. Every year in late July, the wild ponies are rounded up and made to swim the inlet to Chincoteague. They're auctioned to the public. The ones who aren't bought are allowed to swim home.

We were arriving too early for the roundup. Still, I had been dying to see the ponies for myself.

Now, seeing Chincoteague, I was just dying.

I opened my copy of *Misty of Chincoteague* and checked the copyright date.

It read 1947.

"Wow," I murmured. "These books are old."

Jessi nodded. "I guess places change."

Before I could answer, I heard a sudden, loud thud. We all lurched forward.

"What was that?" Abby asked.

Andrew burst into tears. "Did we crash?"

"We were hit," Watson said. He glanced impatiently into the rearview mirror. "Hang on, I'm going to pull over and check the damage."

He steered into a nearby parking lot and edged into a space. The car that had hit us parked in the next space. An older couple and a girl about my age climbed out.

"I am so sorry," the man said to Watson. "Completely my fault."

"My granddad is an excellent driver," the girl announced. "You stopped very abruptly."

"We did not!" Karen protested.

"Now, now," Watson said with a chuckle. "This is a matter for the drivers to settle."

"I'm Saville Hoyer," the man said, extending his hand to Watson. "This is my wife, Judy, and our granddaughter, Felicitas."

Felicitas made a sour face. "*Nobody* calls me that. It's *Liz*."

"We are taking her on a trip to the West Coast," Mrs. Hoyer said. "We are so happy her parents agreed to let her go. . . ."

The grown-ups started walking around to look at the damage, and all us kids followed.

The RV's bumper was dented pretty deeply in the middle.

"Uh-oh," Abby muttered. "What is Watson going to tell the rental place?"

"You could say a wild pony kicked it," Liz suggested. "Wild ponies can be unpredictable."

All the grown-ups laughed, as if that were the cutest thing ever said. Then they started yakking about insurance.

"What have you seen so far?" Liz abruptly asked. "On Chincoteague."

"Well, we just drove in —" I began.

"So far we've seen a snowy egret, a glossy ibis, an osprey, and a Northern bobwhite," Liz barreled on. "You must have seen one of those."

"Uh . . ." said Abby.

"Nahhh, just a bunch of birds and stuff," David Michael piped up.

Liz rolled her eyes. "Those *are* birds. Actually, I came here to see the wild ponies. They're not on Chincoteague Island, you know."

I nodded. "I know. They're on —"

"Assateague," Liz said. "Isn't that the funniest name? Anyway, Marguerite Henry? She's the writer of the *Misty* books? Well, she's wrong about the way the ponies arrived. It wasn't a shipwreck."

"Well, no one knows for sure —" I began.

"The early American settlers? They didn't

have time to build fences, so they used Assateague as a natural pen. You know why? Because it's an island and the horses couldn't escape. Anyway, that's where the wild ponies came from. Actually, they're *feral* ponies. That means their ancestors were domesticated but became wild. And do you know why they look fatter than regular ponies? Because they drink salt water, and that retains moisture in their bodies —"

"All right, Liz! Time to go!" (Saved by the grandmother.)

"'Bye!" Liz said, skipping away. "And don't feed the ponies! It can destroy their natural eating habits."

I looked at Jessi. Her face was twisted into a *I'm-trying-not-to-show-how-annoyed-I-really-am* expression.

"She's either a genius or a robot," David Michael announced.

I cracked up. So did Jessi and Abby. We all climbed back into the RV.

"What a pest!" Jessi said.

"We could hire her as a travel guide," Abby suggested.

I kept my mouth shut. I didn't want to talk about Liz behind her back.

But I could think whatever I wanted. And I sure was glad we didn't have to travel with her.

When we finally started off again, the traffic was moving a little faster. Soon the tourist shops and motels thinned out and disappeared. We were driving over a causeway toward Assateague.

Now *this* was more like it. Assateague was foggy, covered with low pine trees, scrubby plants and grasses, and distant ponds. I reached into my backpack and took out a pair of binoculars I'd brought along. Jessi was already looking through hers. "Do you see anything yet?"

"Just a glossy ibis," Jessi replied. "Or maybe it's a snowy bobwhite."

I raised my binoculars and gazed through them.

A half hour later I was still gazing. My eyes were dry and tired. I'd seen nothing but plants, birds, and water.

"Where did all the horsies go?" Andrew asked.

Abby shrugged. "On a hayride?"

Watson sighed. "We've been twice around the Wildlife Loop. They're supposed to be near here."

"Can't we drive farther out on the island?" I asked.

Watson shook his head. "You need a special permit."

My heart was sinking.

"I'm hungry!" Andrew whined.

"Shall we find a place for a picnic?" Mrs. Brewer asked.

"Yeeeaaa!" shouted David Michael, Andrew, and Karen.

Ahead of us was a sign that read WOODLAND TRAIL/HIKERS AND BIKERS ONLY. Watson maneuvered the RV into a small parking area nearby.

"This is a hiking trail, Watson," Mrs. Brewer said. "The Visitor Center up ahead has picnic facilities."

"It'll be crowded," Watson replied. "Here we can find a nice, open area of our own."

The Brewers had packed us several hampers full of sandwiches and drinks. I threw my binoculars into my pack and slung it over my shoulders. Then I grabbed a hamper and climbed out.

"Bummer, huh?" Jessi said.

"They must have all swum back to Spain," I grumbled.

The trail was more crowded than I expected. And buggy. I must have swatted a hundred mosquitoes. We walked and walked until Andrew started whining. Fortunately we were near a clearing that overlooked a marshy area.

"Well, it's not exactly beachfront," Mrs. Brewer said with a sigh, pulling out a big blanket.

We settled in and began eating. For a moment, I forgot about the ponies. My stomach was growling with hunger. My chicken salad sandwich tasted great. Even if I did have to share it with ants and yellow jackets.

That was when, out of the corner of my eye, I noticed a distant movement.

Beyond the marsh. Over a sand dune.

I grabbed my binoculars.

It was a brown mare nudging along a tiny colt. They stood there a moment, as if they were talking.

Then they were joined by the most beautiful, barrel-chested chestnut I have ever seen.

And another. And another.

"Oh my lord . . ." Abby said.

All at once, the ponies began to run down the dune, kicking up sand.

I dropped my sandwich and stood up.

"Go, Misty!" Jessi cried.

"Horsies!" Andrew screamed.

Mrs. Brewer had tears in her eyes. "They're stunning!"

I didn't say a word. I couldn't.

The sand sprayed up behind them in golden arcs. Their manes were like silky flags, their legs strong and lean.

Exactly the way I'd pictured them.

I just watched until they were out of sight.

Mallory

Until my binoculars were blurry with my own tears.

If the RV were to fall apart, if we had to travel home on a bus, if it rained the rest of the time, it wouldn't matter.

As far as I was concerned, the trip had already been worth it.

CHAPTER 6

Claudia

Wednesday

The Rockin Role Hall of fame was grate.
Exept it didnt have anthing about 44Me
or Blaid. Gess those groops are too new!

Afterword we drov and drov and drov.
I thot the mid west was all close
together. But its not! It goes 4ever!

Now we're near Chicago. Kristy cant
stop talking about Wriggly Field. Stacy
cant stop talking abot Marshal Field. Or
maybe its the other way round. Ones a
baseball park and the others a store.
I'm with Stacy. I will dy if I have to
go to another basball game!! (No ofence,
but I'm glad Mr. Shafer refused to go to
the Pitsberg stadium. 2 far!!!)

Ammmm. I just herd a song on the radio that said Chicago is a toddling town. Sounds like they hav a lot of kids their. Maybe some of us can baby-sit wile Kristys at the game . . .

*K*nock-knock-knock-knock!

"Hurry up! Hurry up! I have to go!"

Jeff's face was red. He twisted the doorknob of the bathroom in the RV.

"I just got in here!" shouted Dawn's voice from inside. "Wait!"

"I can't!"

How many times had I heard this conversation during the ride? About a million.

Let me tell you, a cross-country trip is not for the impatient. Or the claustrophobic.

When we began our trip, the RV seemed like a house on wheels. Beds, a table and chairs, big windows — cool or what? Plus, we had all that free time.

Somewhere outside of Connecticut the house seemed to start shrinking.

I don't know about you, but I can take just so much of sitting still and doing nothing. At first we played cards, but everyone kept beating me. Then we played twenty questions, but I always needed about fifty. I tried sketching the scenery, but it went by too fast and I started feeling sick to my stomach. I listened to the radio, but Mr. Schafer likes to play all this awful old-fashioned music. So I ate an entire bag of Pepperidge Farm Goldfish to console myself. Then I took a long nap.

And that was all in the first two hours.

Three days later, after stops in Cleveland and Detroit, our house on wheels felt like a rolling shoe box. (Smelled like one, too, except you didn't really notice that until you left it and came back.)

During the trip, I discovered a lot of unexpected things about my friends. For instance, I had no idea that Kristy likes to wash her hair with *soap* to "save time" (I nearly fainted). Or that Jeff eats peanut-butter-and-tuna-fish sandwiches. Or that Dawn's organic apples sometimes have worms, which I found out the hard way. Or that the sound of Mary Anne's knitting could drive me absolutely crazy after about two hours.

Tickety-tick-ticka-tickety-tick, went her plastic needles, as Jeff paced the narrow area in front of the bathroom.

When Mary Anne first started knitting, the sound reminded me of soft rain on a cozy night. After awhile, it was like mice skittering on a tile floor.

Now I was thinking about skeleton bones rattling in a grave.

"Uh, Mary Anne?" I began.

Click. The bathroom door swung open.

Jeff dived in practically before Dawn had a chance to escape. He slammed the door behind him.

"He always waits until the last minute," Dawn grumbled.

"What's the difference?" Jeff's voice shouted from inside. "No matter when I want to go, you're always in there!"

"Chicago, fifty-seven miles!" Mr. Schafer announced.

"Oh, groan," I groaned. "Another hour."

"Patience, Claudia," said Stacey, who was sitting in the seat behind Mr. Schafer, gazing listlessly out the window.

Mary Anne looked up from her knitting. "My dad goes to Chicago a lot for his law firm. He loves it there."

"Ah, wining and dining away from home on an expense account, eh?" Mr. Schafer said with a chuckle. "Must be nice."

"He works very hard," Mary Anne replied. "It's not really a vacation —"

"My lawyer friends are all workaholics," Mr. Schafer said. "They never see their families. That's one thing I like about my job. Evenings and weekends are mine."

Tickety-tickticktickticktick! Mary Anne was going double time now. "Actually, my dad spends lots of time with us," she mumbled.

"I'm sure he does —"

"Hey, Chicago has a beach!" cried Kristy, looking up from a travel guide. "It's right in the city!"

"Surf's up!" Dawn yelled.

Jeff burst out of the bathroom. "Can we go there? I mean, after the ball game?"

"The Cubs are away today," Kristy informed him. "We're just going to look at the stadium and buy a cap."

"Maybe we can stop at the beach on the way to the Art Institute," Mr. Schafer said.

Jeff's face fell. "*Art Institute?* Do we have to?"

"Dad promised Claudia," Dawn reminded him.

"It has the *best* Impressionist collection," I added.

Kristy eagerly leafed through her book. "How about Lincoln Park Zoo? Or the Bicycle Museum, Chicago Children's Museum, Field Museum of Natural History —"

"Yyyyyesss!" Jeff said. "All of them."

Mr. Schafer exhaled. "It's lunchtime. Let's stop, and then we can negotiate."

He drove off the highway and found a multi-purpose fast-food place (with a salad bar for Dawn, of course). As we pulled into a space, my mouth was watering. I unbuckled my belt and quickly went over to my bunk bed to fetch my wallet. My backpack was sprawled on top of the unmade sheets, and I reached for it.

At the edge of the bed I saw a small spiral notebook. I'd brought along a couple of them, with unlined pages for doodling. But this one didn't look familiar. I opened it up and saw some handwriting:

We stopped in Detroit today. Why? Another baseball stadium, of course. But we had fun anyway. I ♥ed the food in Greektown !! YUM ! And I bought these FABULOUS earrings in Trappers Alley . . .

Oops. Stacey's book, not mine. It must have fallen from her bunk above. I shut the book and reached upward.

"What are you doing?"

I turned. Stacey was standing behind me, hands on hips.

"Here," I said. "This is yours."

She grabbed the book out of my hands. "No kidding. Find anything interesting?"

"I wasn't reading it, Stacey —"

"Just looking at the artwork, huh?" Stacey snapped.

"But — but —"

She flew out the door, leaving me alone in the RV.

Great. We weren't even halfway across the country and my best friend was mad at me.

This trip had already been too long.

I didn't know how we were going to make it to California in one piece.

Well, Stacey didn't talk to me in the fast-food restaurant. I tried to explain what had happened, but she wouldn't listen. It didn't help that Jeff, the gossip-in-training, kept asking me to recite every word I'd read.

The trip into Chicago was grim. Stacey kept her back to me the whole time. Mary Anne knitted her fingers off. Dawn and Jeff fought. Kristy seemed oblivious to the whole thing and kept reading aloud from her guidebook.

Just inside the Chicago city limits, on the highway alongside Lake Michigan, we hit a horrible traffic jam. How horrible? I was able to make a detailed sketch of the Chicago skyline.

Since the Art Institute was closer, Mr. Schafer decided to drive off the highway and stop there first. I won't even tell you Jeff's reaction. (My hearing has still not recovered.)

No matter. The Art Institute was fantastic! It's one thing to admire paintings in a book, but seeing them live is an entirely different experience. Like eating chocolate for the first time after hearing someone describe the taste.

At least that was how I explained it to Jeff. His response? "Can we go now?"

"How about the arms and armor exhibit?" Mr. Schafer suggested.

Jeff and Kristy liked that idea. Stacey and Dawn wanted to go to the gift shop. We all agreed to meet at the front entrance in two hours.

The only one who stayed to look at the paintings with me was Mary Anne. "My dad loves the Impressionist collection," she said softly as we wandered among the Monets. "He's only been here once, though. He really doesn't have the time."

"Too bad," I said.

"I mean, with his work schedule and all. He really does work so hard."

I thought about Mary Anne's conversation with Mr. Schafer in the RV.

"I believe you, Mary Anne," I said. "You were really taking Mr. Schafer's jokes seriously, huh?"

"I guess."

We passed silently from room to room. We had a couple of hours before leaving for Wrigley Field, and I think we were both happy for the quiet. And the space.

Abby

Thursday
Memphis
Hometown of THE KING

I am crushed.
Devastated.
I am taking up
residence in the
Heartbreak Hotel.
Why didn't I look
it up in advance?
Why didn't I call?
If I had, I might
have been able to
postpone our trip.
I might have convin-
ced Watson and Mr.
Schafer to drive
cross-country a few

precious days later.
Then we would be
Pulling into memphis
at the right time.
    But were not.
We're missing ELVIS
WEEK . . . .

"It's him!" Karen screamed.

She stared at her Graceland pamphlet, then back out the RV window.

"It's who?" I asked.

"Elvis! Look! In that pink car!"

I pasted my face to the window.

I could not believe what I was seeing. A pink Cadillac. Exactly the kind of car the King used to drive. Unfortunately, it was making a turn onto a side road, and I couldn't see who was in it.

"The King," by the way, is Elvis. In case you haven't guessed. As far as I'm concerned, the King rules.

I know I should say *ruled*. Most people believe Elvis is dead. But not everyone. I've read about so many Elvis sightings in the tabloids while waiting in the supermarket checkout line. I ask you, can they *all* be wrong?

Sure they can. But it's fun to think they're right.

On the way down to Memphis, I presented my case to everyone in the RV. Jessi was still skeptical, and I could tell Watson and Mrs. Brewer were just tolerating me, but I was working on Mallory.

The little ones — David Michael, Karen, and Andrew — were with me all the way.

Abby

Now, early in the morning (after a night at a campsite and breakfast at a diner), we were heading straight for THE PLACE. The number-one most important stop of the trip: Elvis's estate, Graceland.

Well, not all of us. Watson announced that he and Mrs. Brewer needed "time off." He agreed to drop us kids at Graceland while they went to take a tour of a World War II bomber. (Hey, there's no accounting for taste.)

Why do I love Elvis so much? He's retro. He's cool. His voice is amazing. And those eyes! That smile! (Forget about those pictures of him as a fat, middle-aged guy in a white leisure suit. Look at the film clips of him when he was starting out. Whoa.)

Anyway, at the diner that morning, I had picked up lots of Graceland brochures. That was when I found out about Elvis Week.

"What's a candlelight vye gill?" David Michael asked, looking up from one of the brochures.

I turned away from the window. "Vigil. It happens on the night of August fifteenth, during Elvis Week. People march with candles past his grave, to commemorate the day he died."

"But we just saw him!" Karen insisted.

Andrew's face was pale. "He was a skeleton, driving the car?"

"No, he was alive," Karen insisted. "Really. He looked just like the picture."

"He's a *ghost*?" Andrew whimpered.

"Uh, kids, can we drop the subject?" Mrs. Brewer asked.

"'There are almost five hundred Elvis fan clubs worldwide,'" Karen read. "'If you put all of Elvis's albums ever sold end to end, they would circle the earth twice. . . .'"

We heard Elvis trivia all the way to the entrance of Graceland.

I was amazed when I saw the place up close. It's huge. It makes Kristy's mansion look like a pup tent.

And people were lined up around the block to get in.

"Are they giving away free burgers?" Watson joked.

"Good thing we made reservations," I said.

"It's only a dumb *house*," David Michael remarked. "Can't we see the bomber instead?"

Watson said a quick no to that suggestion. "We'll pick you up at one o'clock, in the parking lot of the mall across the street. If you're done early, have lunch there."

He let us out near the end of the line and drove off.

About an hour later, we were inside. Breathing the same air Elvis had breathed. Walking on the same carpet.

We took a guided tour and then wandered on our own. Frankly, Elvis's taste was pretty gaudy. I thought the jungle decor in his den was a little strange, but I did like the hall decorated floor to ceiling with gold records.

Jessi and Mallory liked it, too. And David Michael walked around singing "Jailhouse Rock" at the top of his lungs. But Karen lost interest, and Andrew started whining with hunger pains.

As we left, I glanced at my watch. It was 12:20.

"We have half an hour," I announced. "How about lunch?"

"YEAAAA!" It was unanimous. We were off to the mall across the street from Graceland.

Except Karen. She was standing still, looking back toward the mansion.

"There it is again!" she cried out.

I turned. A pink Cadillac was driving slowly away from Graceland. The same one we had seen on the way in.

"Hold up, guys!" I said.

David Michael let out a loud sigh. "A yucky pink car. So?"

The Cadillac circled the grounds. It came to a

stop outside a motel near the shopping center. The door opened, and out climbed the driver.

My jaw dropped so fast it nearly hit the sidewalk.

It was HIM.

The King himself.

His hair was jet black and moussed back on the sides. He was thick around the middle — okay, fat — and was wearing a white, rhinestone-studded jumpsuit, with matching wraparound sunglasses.

He took a large box out of the backseat of his car. Walking briskly with it toward the motel, he glanced our way.

He flashed a smile. Well, more like a half smile with a curled upper lip.

I froze. I'd seen that smile a million times, in photos and movies. Pure Elvis.

"He saw us!" Karen exclaimed.

"He looks just like Elvers," Andrew remarked.

"Too old and fat," David Michael said.

"He was chubby in those photos before he died," I spoke up. "Or supposedly died. That was in nineteen seventy-seven."

"So he *is* a ghost!" Andrew exclaimed.

"Some people say he's still alive," Mallory said, "but he wants people to think he's dead."

"Why?" David Michael asked.

"So he can have his privacy," Karen explained.

Andrew looked confused. "Can't he just close the bathroom door?"

"Come on," I said, grabbing Andrew's hand. "Let's see where he's going."

"This is ridiculous," Jessi said.

Jessi was outnumbered. We all scurried to the corner and crossed the street. The side of the motel came into view. Elvis was standing in the shadow of the building, lowering his box to the ground.

He knocked on the nearest door. It opened a moment later, and Elvis picked up the box and walked in.

"Why is he staying *there*?" Karen asked.

"Maybe he's delivering something to his neighbors," Mallory said. "Remember what the tour guide said? Elvis always gave stuff freely to friends and family and poor people."

"I don't believe this," Jessi murmured.

"Let's knock on the door!" David Michael suggested.

"That's silly," Karen said. "Besides, if he's just delivering something, he'll come out anyway."

We were inching toward the Cadillac. "What if he does come out?" Jessi whispered. "What are we going to do?"

Click!

The motel door flew open again. My legs locked.

Out came Elvis. Behind him was another man.

This one had slicked-back black hair, too. But he was younger and thinner, and he wore a fifties-style jacket.

Behind him was . . . another Elvis, carrying a guitar case.

And another.

Last of all was a balding man in a business suit, with a stack of flyers. He smiled and handed a flyer and a business card to me. "Hi, there! Come see us!"

Jessi, Mallory, David Michael, Karen, and Andrew all gathered around as I read aloud the words on the flyer: "'Elvis International Impersonator Contest, August 11–14 . . .'"

"Still alive, huh?" Jessi said, raising an eyebrow.

"He was a *fake*?" David Michael asked.

"Well, uh, yeah," I said. "I mean, I never *really* believed he was alive."

Which was true. Sort of.

Jessi started howling. David Michael joined her. Then Mallory and Karen and Andrew.

As for me? If you can't beat 'em, join 'em.

Okay, so the King is dead.

That doesn't mean you have to stop looking.

CHAPTER 8

MaryAnne

Thursday

Something's wrong with the RV. It's riding way too low to the ground. And it's not because of the luggage.

Guys, I think we ate too much at the original Pizzeria Uno in Chicago!

Just kidding. But we really have to keep our appetites down before we visit Maynard. Otherwise we may not have enough room for my grandma's cooking! (She is the best cook I've ever met.)

Oh, well. We have time. We can fast on the way....

"Hi, Grandma!" I said into the pay phone.

"Mary Anne, dear! How lovely to hear your voice," my grandmother replied. "Where are you?"

I was standing in a phone bank in a place called the Woodfield Mall. Stacey had heard someone talking about it when we were in Water Tower Place in Chicago.

This mall looked a lot like the other mall, except bigger.

Frankly, I was growing tired of malls. Ballparks, too. I couldn't wait for a nice, quiet visit to Maynard.

"I'm in Shaumberg, Illinois," I said. "I wanted to call to tell you we're going to be a day late. There was so much to do in Chicago that we stayed an extra day. I hope you don't mind."

"Oh, that's just as well, dear," Grandma said. "The painters are still working on the house. It's a dreadful mess. In fact, I was thinking of meeting you at a restaurant. Although the restaurants in Maynard may not seem so wonderful compared to Chicago. So when will you be here?"

"Well, first my friend Kristy wants to see the Milwaukee Brewers' baseball stadium — Brewer is her stepfamily's name — and then the stadium in Minneapolis —"

"The Metrodome? Terrific. You know, your

grandfather was a Twins fan. We saw many a game there."

"Well, don't worry, we're only stopping long enough for Kristy to buy a baseball cap. Then we're going straight to Maynard."

"No," Grandma said abruptly.

"No?"

"No. Let me meet you in Minneapolis. This is your vacation, Mary Anne. Why should you go all the way north to Minnesota then rush all the way down to Iowa?"

"Well . . . isn't it out of the way for you?"

Grandma chuckled. "A few hours in a car doesn't faze us Midwesterners, Mary Anne. Besides, my house is a shambles, and I need a good excuse to get away. Now, where could we meet that you all might enjoy?"

"Well, I don't know the city. . . ."

"I know the perfect place! You'll just love it! It's in Bloomington, just outside the city. Do you think your driver would make the trip?"

"Sure!" It would be so much fun to visit an out-of-the-way place that someone actually knew!

"It's called the Mall of America," Grandma continued. "Meet me at the entrance to Camp Snoopy."

I could feel the blood draining from my face. "A *mall*?"

"The biggest and best you've ever seen."

I swallowed. Suddenly the sights and sounds of the Woodfield Mall were crowding in on me. I watched a little boy throw a temper tantrum outside an ice-cream store. Through the speakers I could hear the dreadful Muzak version of an old Madonna song. I wanted to scream.

"Okay, Grandma," I said. "We're supposed to arrive in Minnesota the day after tomorrow. I'll call with an exact time."

"I can't wait!"

"Me, neither."

I hung up.

I felt awful.

Why couldn't I have insisted on going to Maynard? How selfish of me to make her travel all the way to Minneapolis, just to go to a mall.

It was her suggestion, I told myself. Maybe she had a good reason. Besides, I should be grateful and happy that I was seeing her at all.

I bought absolutely nothing at the Woodfield Mall. Stacey and Claudia were pretty restrained, too — mainly because Mr. Schafer told them the RV had no more room.

On the ride to Wisconsin, the RV was very quiet. Stacey and Claudia weren't talking to each other. Kristy, Dawn, Jeff, and I played a low-energy card game the whole way.

After awhile, Mr. Schafer began cracking jokes and trying to start sing-alongs.

That was about the last thing I wanted. As far as I was concerned, that just added to the tension.

Now, I don't mean to be a spoilsport. I know Mr. Schafer meant well. And I appreciated how patient and flexible he was. I'm sure it's not easy to be the only grown-up in an RV full of kids.

But Mr. Schafer is one of those adults who likes to say teasing things — about the East Coast, for instance, or about Stoneybrook. Or about my dad.

I thought I knew Mr. Schafer pretty well. I was a bridesmaid in his wedding. Back then, Jeff was going through a stand-up comedian phase. He couldn't stop joking, even after everyone's patience faded.

Now I knew where that came from.

I do have a sense of humor. I can laugh about myself just fine. But Mr. Schafer was going overboard, just like Jeff. I couldn't help wondering why. Was he mad at Sharon for marrying Dad? Was he mad at me?

Ease up, I kept telling myself. *It's just the pressure of the long trip.*

We stayed overnight in Milwaukee, because Kristy wanted to see a Brewers game. Outside the stadium, Dawn began lecturing a vendor who was serving bratwurst ("stuffed animal entrails," she called it).

We spent Friday exploring the city, then drove straight to an RV park in the woods of Minnesota. On Saturday we headed straight for Bloomington — and the Mall of America.

What was it like? Pretty cool, actually. Camp Snoopy is an amusement park in the center of the mall. It has rides and a roller coaster.

We were half an hour late, but Grandma was waiting patiently by the Camp Snoopy entrance.

"Hiiiii!" I cried out, running into her arms.

"My baby!" Grandma said.

We hugged and hugged. All my strange, tense feelings that had built up during the trip were flying away.

I introduced everyone. The first thing Grandma asked was, "Lunch first, or rides?"

The rides won out. We went on the roller coaster and the Ferris wheel and the Mystery Mine Ride. We even rode the train. It was a blast.

Well, I guess there are malls and there are *malls*.

After awhile, we were starving. Dawn led us all to — what else? — a health food restaurant. She made us order food we'd never heard of. I

had "succulent sautéed seitan cutlets." Seitan is wheat gluten. It's supposed to taste like steak.

It doesn't.

I must have made a face while I was eating the seitan, because Mr. Schafer laughed at me. "Used to that heavy red-meat diet, huh?" he asked.

I smiled. "I guess."

"Oh?" Dawn raised an eyebrow. "Have you gone back to red meat since I've left Stoneybrook?"

"Old Richard seems like a meat-and-potatoes guy," Mr. Schafer said with a chuckle.

"He's not," I said. "Maybe once or twice a week."

I could feel my face burning. Why was he doing this in front of my own grandmother?

"My son-in-law," Grandma said sweetly, "eats very, very well. In fact, judging from that little belly of yours, you could take a tip from him."

The whole table cracked up. Mr. Schafer smiled sheepishly and dug into his lunch.

I could barely keep from laughing.

It was great to see Grandma again. Mall or no mall.

CHAPTER 9

Jessi

Friday
Dalton, Mississippi

We made it. We are in the Dalton Plantation Museum! Well, not all of us. Abby, Mallory, and I, to be exact. David Michael, Karen, and Andrew are at McDonald's with Watson and Mrs. Brewer. Which is just as well. The fine print in the museum brochure reads, "Some images

94

inside may not
be suitable for
young viewers."
I wonder exactly
how young they
mean?

Jessi

"The Dalton family owned approximately seven thousand acres," the tour guide said in a blasé voice, "as far as the eye can see, in all directions, and farther. Much of the land was sold, and it became the towns of Dalton and Wainwright."

Abby let out a low whistle. "A backyard big enough to fit two towns. I'm impressed."

Impressed wasn't the word. *Knocked out* was more like it. The Dalton museum was absolutely humongous. We were on the porch, which was lined with white columns as tall as trees. The floor was wide enough to stage a ballet. You could fit three Gracelands inside the building.

"How many families lived here?" Mallory asked.

The guide smiled. "Just the Daltons. The household servants, too, behind the kitchen and in the attic. Out back, just hidden by the trees, are the slave quarters."

She pointed vaguely toward a nearby field, then led us into the house. "The Daltons had one of the largest cotton plantations in Mississippi. They kept approximately one hundred slaves. . . ."

I raised my hand. "Are there records of the slave families?"

"In a way," the guide said. "The slaves were considered possessions, so some of them are mentioned in household account books and bills of sale. Unfortunately, the owners referred to their slaves only by first names, so it's just about impossible to know who they were. The Daltons were known for humane treatment of slaves, however. . . ."

Humane treatment? How could the Daltons be humane if they considered slaves "possessions" and only allowed them one name — like pets? And what about the slaves themselves? Didn't they keep their own records?

I wanted to ask a million questions. But I felt self-conscious. For one thing, Abby, Mallory, and I were the only kids in the tour group. And among the fifteen or so others, only one older couple was African-American.

The guide was now moving through the first floor. "To the right," she droned on, "we have the Louis the Fourteenth room, many elements of which the Vanderbilts copied for their famous estate in North Carolina. . . ."

I spun around slowly to take it all in. The walls were covered with photos of stiff-looking people — stiff, bored children in tight, frilly clothes; stiff, grim men with handlebar mustaches sitting on horses; stiff women with ringleted hair and hoopskirts. The Daltons.

The people my ancestors lived with.

The people my ancestors were *owned by*.

That's what being a slave meant. You could be bought and sold. Like a mule.

What must it have been like to leave Africa and come to a place like this? What were my ancestors' tribal names? Where did they work? What did they look like?

It didn't seem as if I would find out anything here. The tour guide was leading us from one fancy room to another. I saw more satin, lace, and brocaded curtains than I'd seen in my entire life.

After we'd explored the bedrooms upstairs, the guide led us up a plain wooden staircase into the attic. Up there, I broke into an instant sweat. The hot, stuffy air was almost like soup.

We walked into a cluster of dark, teeny rooms. Small beds with thin, lumpy mattresses stood close together on a plain wooden floor. The slanted roof beams overhead were studded with sharp, rusty nails.

"The household servants slept up here," the guide said, then pointed to a contraption on the wall that held several different-sized bells. "The signaling system was considered very modern. Members of the Dalton family would press a button in one of the rooms downstairs to summon a servant, and through an electrical connection, it would ring up here. The servants were on call twenty-four hours a day, seven days a week."

Abby sneezed. This place was Allergy City.

"Yuck," Mallory said.

My stomach was sinking.

The guide led us back down the narrow stairway. At the bottom, we explored the main kitchen, then went through a screen door into the yard.

A walkway led to a barnlike building. Over its front door was a plaque that read SLAVERY AT THE DALTON PLANTATION.

The inside had been renovated into a modern exhibit hall. Mannequins in raggedy clothes were frozen in work positions — bent over ironing, serving from huge pots, picking cotton.

Along the wall were framed drawings and photographs from the 1800s. Some of the drawings were crude cartoons from local newspapers, showing the bigoted attitudes that existed. But the old photos of the slaves told another, more human story. Almost all of them showed the slaves in the field — dozens of them hunched over the cotton plants. But a few of the pictures were portraits. Beneath the cracks and scratches, the faces expressed so much. Some looked defiant and proud, others haunted and afraid.

Not one photo was labeled with a name. I stared into every face. I tried to see resemblances to the Ramsey family, but it was hopeless.

Soon I came to a section marked MAN'S INHUMANITY TO MAN. First I saw a sketched diagram of a slave ship. Slaves were packed like sardines, one slave's head next to another's feet. Then I saw a drawing of a slave auction. An African man stood on a platform with a chain around his neck, like a prize steer at a county fair. Disgusting.

Then I came to a photograph of a lynching, and I almost gagged. A slave, a young man, was hanging from a tree. Around him was a whole crowd of white people. Some were pointing calmly. Others were smirking. A few children were among them, just staring.

Children!

No one back then warned about "unsuitable images."

I was feeling sick.

The tour group was on the opposite side of the room. I went up to Mallory and nudged her. "I'm going to take a walk. Be right back."

Outside, the fresh air calmed me down.

I walked down a slope and onto a small grassy field. Probably a cotton field at one time, I figured.

Once I read a book, *Time and Again*, in which a character surrounds himself with stuff from the 1800s and is able to imagine himself into the past. Of course, I don't believe that can happen. But sometimes, when no one is looking, I squint my eyes and try to do the same thing.

A few tourists were strolling by a grove of willow trees, but I turned away from them. I looked at the open field and squinted.

I pictured rows and rows of cotton. I imagined slaves moving through those rows, stooped over. Tall, sturdy women with kerchiefs wrapped around their heads, bent, hobbled old people; small, quick-moving children . . .

My eyes were watering. I saw my whole family out there — Grandma and Grandpa, Daddy, Mama, Aunt Cecelia, my little sister, Becca . . .

"Are you lost, darling?"

The voice startled me. I whirled around. Standing behind me was a smiling African-American woman. Her hair was flecked with gray and she was wearing glasses. She wore a breezy plaid summer dress, and her right arm was folded around a couple of hardcover books.

"No!" I said with a gasp. "Just . . . exploring."

"Sorry if I scared you," the woman said. "I'm Annie Pardell."

She extended her hand and I shook it. "Jessica Ramsey. I'm here with some friends. They're on the guided tour. I was just looking at the slavery exhibit."

"You don't sound like you live around here."

"No. Stoneybrook, Connecticut. But my family used to work on this plantation. At least that's what my grandparents told me." I sighed. "I was hoping to find out some information about them."

"Well, we have a lot in common," Ms. Pardell said as we began walking slowly through the grass together. "My family worked here, too."

"Really? So we might be related?"

Ms. Pardell laughed. "Who knows? I'm here for the summer doing some doctoral research on the Mississippi slave trade. Let me tell you, Jessica, it's almost impossible to find specific genealogical information on slave families."

"Didn't anyone write anything down?"

"Honey, in the eyes of the plantation owners, an educated slave was a rebellious slave. Reading or writing was banned."

"Couldn't they teach each other at night or something?"

"Some did, but there weren't too many who could do the teaching." Ms. Pardell gestured toward the willow trees. From our angle, I could see a group of small wooden shacks. "That's a replica of where the slaves lived. Back then, the willows weren't there, so Mr. Dalton could spy

on his slaves any time he wanted to. If you needed to pass along a secret — some news of the Underground Railroad, say — you did it on the sly."

"What happened if you were caught?"

Ms. Pardell sighed. "Well, you saw those awful photographs in the exhibit. You avoided capture at all costs. But there were ways to pass on information. One thing you did was sing. See, the owners didn't mind that. They figured singing kept up the work spirit. What they didn't know was that many of those songs were in code. Have you ever heard the song 'Follow the Drinking Gourd'? Well, the words told about a secret escape route for the Underground Railroad, in the direction of the Big Dipper . . . the drinking gourd! The slaves would pass the song on from plantation to plantation." She began singing softly: "For the old man is waitin' for to carry you to freedom if you follow the drinking gourd . . ."

I listened to her soft voice. If I concentrated, I could hear the song rising up from the field, the voices of the slaves carrying it to the horizon.

We walked silently for awhile. I knew I'd have to rejoin my friends soon. I also knew I'd probably never learn about the Ramsey family. I thought about the slave ship. The lynching photo. The generations of slave workers in the fields.

Somehow, though, I kept thinking about the singing. And the slaves who escaped. Maybe my great-great-great-great-grandparents were among them.

"Thanks, Ms. Pardell," I said. "I'd better go."

We shook hands and said good-bye. As I walked away, I saw her wandering farther and farther into the field. Humming.

CHAPTER 10

Dawn

Sunday
Badlands, South Dakota

Is this a strange name or what? I mean, if I were the governor of South Dakota, and I wanted people to visit my state, would I call a national park area BADlands? No way! I know some areas of Los Angeles that would fit that description better. . . .

"**I** want to go to Wind Cave National Park!" Kristy announced, passing around a South Dakota booklet. "It has one of the longest caves in the world."

"Ooh! Ooh! Ooh! Flintstones, Bedrock City!" Jeff blurted out. "Yabba-dabba-doooo!"

I rolled my eyes. "Let's not and say we yabba-dabba-did."

"How about Mount Rushmore?" Dad suggested.

Stacey took the brochure and squinted at a photo. "'The Corn Palace,'" she read, "'decorated with giant murals made of colored corn, grains, and grasses.' Weird."

"Ooh, the Laura Ingalls Wilder home," Mary Anne said, looking over Stacey's shoulder.

"Who's that?" Jeff asked.

"The author who wrote *Little House on the Prairie*," Mary Anne replied.

"Girls are boring," Jeff murmured.

Please excuse my brother's rudeness. Tempers were a bit short in our RV. Too short, in my opinion. I didn't know what was bugging Claudia and Stacey. They weren't even looking at each other. Mary Anne was being grumpy for no reason whatsoever. And Kristy was mad because we were heading into a baseball-free zone.

Dawn

To tell you the truth, I had not been looking forward to South Dakota. I mean, say New York and I imagine skyscrapers, noise, excitement. California? Beaches, surfing, movies. Ohio has the Rock and Roll Hall of Fame, Illinois has Chicago. But South Dakota? A big fat *nada*.

Well, I was wrong. I hadn't heard so much excitement in the RV since we left the Mall of America.

Finally, Dad pulled over to a rest stop. We looked at a map and decided that since we were running a little late, we'd make one major stop. We were all leaning toward Mount Rushmore when Jeff found something new in the brochure.

"'Mammoth Site!'" he cried out. "They have woolly mammoth fossils still in the ground and you can touch them. I *have* to go to this!"

Cool. We all agreed.

One problem. To reach it, you had to drive across the whole state. A very, very long state. With lots of farms.

Now, I have nothing against farms, but to a suburban girl like me, they can start to look alike after awhile.

That would have been fine if we had a few car games going, or some singing, or even a decent radio station.

But even cheerful old Dad had given up trying.

I fell asleep looking at a flat prairie.

I woke up on the moon.

I had to blink. I thought I was dreaming.

The farms were gone. Outside the window, the landscape was rocky and dry. Between long, flat stretches, jagged peaks rose up. They looked like the outstretched fingers of underground rock monsters trying to burst through the surface.

Aside from Dad, I was the only person awake in the RV.

"Where *are* we?" I asked.

"The badlands," Dad replied. "The early settlers feared this area more than any other."

"So what are we doing here?"

Dad smiled. "I thought it would be a nice sightseeing detour. Too bad no one else is awa —"

He cut himself off. He was staring at his dashboard. The RV was slowing down.

"Why are you stopping?" I asked.

"I'm not." Dad dropped his head to the steering wheel and groaned. "We're out of gas."

"*Whaaaaaaat?*"

"How could I be so stupid?" Dad said.

"What are we going to do now?" I was trying not to scream. Really. But I couldn't help it.

In the seat behind me, Jeff was stirring. "Are we there yet?"

"Washington, D.C.! All out!" Claudia called out in a half yawn.

"Claudia, this is no joke," I said. "We ran out of gas!"

"WE'RE OUT OF GAS?" That was Kristy. She was awake now, too.

"Don't panic!" Dad said in a panicked voice, grabbing a map from the dashboard. "I'll get us out of here."

Jeff was wailing. Kristy and Stacey started arguing about what to do. Mary Anne was sniffling. Claudia had pulled her pad out and was sketching the landscape.

Around a corner ahead, a Jeep came whizzing toward us. It was the first vehicle I'd seen since I awoke.

"HEEEYYYY!" Dad climbed out and flagged it down.

A man and woman and two children were inside. We all plastered our faces to the window as Dad leaned in and talked to the grown-ups.

When he turned back to us, he looked grim. "Okay, east of here is a place called Cedar Pass. I'm going to catch a ride with this couple and —"

"Hitch a ride?" I was mortified. "What about us?"

110

"Look, I'm not happy about it myself, but I don't see any other choice, and Mr. Kingman here says we won't take long. So you lock up the RV, flag down a trooper if you see one, and I will try to race back."

What could we do? We all nodded.

Mary Anne choked back a sob. It was infectious. I did, too. Jeff had folded himself on the seat, hiding his head.

"Okay, baseball trivia quiz!" Kristy blurted out. "What Chicago Cub holds the record for —"

"Kristy, how can you think of baseball at a time like this?" Claudia threw down her pad. "Look at this place. I mean, the dark doesn't scare me. Horror movies don't scare me. New York City doesn't scare me. But I can't even draw this place without being scared!"

Kristy shrugged. "A game might calm you down."

We argued. We complained. We eventually played Kristy's game. Then we played twenty questions about twenty times. Then we made a list of every single thing we'd seen on the trip.

When the sun began to set, we ran out of things to do. So we fell silent and watched.

In the sharp angle of the sun's light, the peaks threw long, pointed shadows across the badlands. Shadows that seemed to reach toward us.

"How long has he been gone?" Jeff finally asked.

I looked at my watch. "Over an hour and a half."

"Hey, I know a great round to sing," I said.

As I began teaching my friends "By the Waters of Babylon," the sun went down over a distant peak.

Night was falling. And Dad was nowhere in sight.

CHAPTER 11

Abby

Sunday

Yeeeeeee-hah!
We're in Oklahoma,
podners, and on
our way to a real,
live, dang-nabbed,
whip-crackin'
rodeo!

What on earth is a podner?

Hyeh, hyeh, hyeh.
If ya dunno, Miz
Pike, ya mus' be
some kinda tender-
foot.

Abby, you are so weird.

Mebbe. But first, folks, we're gonna rustle up some grub in the beautiful, newfangled metropolis of Lester. ...

"W<small>AAAAAAHHHHHH</small>!"

That was our greeting at the home of Chet and Linda Romney.

Actually, the greeting was from a teeny baby in the arms of a smiling, brown-haired woman who answered the doorbell.

"Welcome, I'm Linda," the woman said. "And this is Isabella."

As Watson and Mrs. Brewer introduced themselves, a heavyset, balding man appeared. When he saw Watson, he beamed.

"Heeeyyyyy, buddy," he said, giving Watson a bear hug. "The last time I saw you, you used a comb, not a shoe-shine kit!"

Watson laughed. "Oh, low blow! Look who's talking!"

"WAAAAAAHHHHHH!" repeated the baby.

"May I hold her?" Jessi, Mallory, and I asked at the same time.

Mrs. Romney laughed. "Yes, yes, and yes. Come on in and sit down."

At long last, on a cool, cloudy day, we'd arrived in the heart of Lester, Oklahoma. Which is not, by the way, a metropolis. Or beautiful or newfangled. But Chet Romney was Watson's college roommate at Baylor University, and they had not seen each other in ten years. And *that's* why we were visiting Lester.

Abby

Briefly visiting.

To be honest, I was itching to see a rodeo almost as much as David Michael was. Our trip was starting to feel very long. We hadn't had a major stop since the Dalton Plantation Museum. All through Arkansas and Oklahoma, Andrew had been whining, "Are we in California yet?"

For most of that time, Jessi and Mal had been busily writing. Mal thought Jessi's experience at Dalton would make a dramatic children's book.

Personally, I become carsick if I look at a page of anything in a moving vehicle. So I was feeling pretty restless as we walked into the Romney house.

"You picked the coolest day of the summer!" Mr. Romney said. "I was hoping we'd barbecue outside, but we'll just have to settle for in here."

Settle? As we sat around the living room, playing with Isabella, Mr. Romney brought in enough munchies to feed a houseful of Claudias. Lunch was chicken-fried steak, thick cheeseburgers, corn on the cob, potato salad, and about a dozen other courses.

We were in pig heaven. David Michael's plate was piled so high you could barely see him. Andrew was so excited he started eating with his hands. (Jessi, Mallory, and I were much more civilized. Ahem.) Karen could not stop giggling about the name "chicken-fried steak." She said it made her picture a live chicken frying a T-bone at the stove.

What a feast. I was full halfway through. Mr. and Mrs. Romney were sitting across from me, happily chatting away, with Isabella between them.

I sat back and gazed out the window. The sky looked so interesting now. Sort of greenish. The clouds had flattened into a dark, narrow band.

Picking up my spoon, I noticed my arm hairs were standing up. I smoothed them down.

"Are you cold, Abby?" Mrs. Brewer asked.

Now my scalp was feeling prickly, too. I laughed. "No. But it's so weird. My hair feels funny."

Mr. Romney cut himself off in the middle of a sentence and cast a glance toward me. Then he turned around to look out the window. "Excuse me," he muttered.

He hurried into the living room. From my angle, I could see him flick on the TV. An old movie lit up the screen. Across the bottom, in large white letters, were the words TORNADO WATCH UPGRADED TO A WARNING.

"*Tornado?*" I blurted out.

We all practically jumped out of our seats.

Now Mr. and Mrs. Romney were standing at the window, looking at the band of clouds. "It

117

sure looks like it," Mr. Romney murmured. "Well, Watson, old buddy, we Oklahomans sure know how to welcome out-of-towners, huh?"

"This is no time to joke," Mrs. Romney said, running to lift Isabella from her high chair. "A warning is very serious. Let's take shelter."

Andrew's little face crumpled. "Are we going to get blowed away?"

"Just like Dorothy — dee-dee-dee-dee-dee-deeeeee-dee!" David Michael sang, in his best attempt at Miss Gulch's theme from *The Wizard of Oz.*

"Do you have a cellar?" Karen asked.

"No," Mr. Romney said, quickly clearing the table. "We'll have to use the bathroom. Go ahead. I'll be there in a minute."

Mrs. Brewer lifted Andrew off his seat. "We're using the bathroom together?" he asked.

"Not that kind of using the bathroom!" Karen exclaimed. "We have to hide from the twister!"

"WAAAAAAHHHHHH!" cried Isabella.

"WAAAAAAHHHHHH!" cried Andrew.

Into the bathroom everyone ran. Except me. I was staring out the window. At the greenish cloud cover.

It was now like a thick, dark blanket across the sky. Four pointy, twitching funnels were growing downward from it, as if four giant, gray puppies were sitting above the clouds and their waggly tails were poking through.

One of the ones in the middle was growing longer and longer. I could hear a noise now, a low rumble like an approaching freight train.

"Abigail!" shouted Mrs. Brewer's voice from inside.

"Come on!" That was Mr. Romney. He took me by the elbow and firmly guided me away from the window. Under his left arm were two large pillows from the living room sofa. In his hand was a portable radio. "You're in the worst place! If it hits — or comes close — the windows might blow inward!"

We raced toward the bathroom. "What's that noise?" I shouted.

"The twister!"

"You're kidding!"

Mr. Romney didn't answer. But he had a definite not-kidding look on his face.

I was about to ask him about the pillows. But I heard a fit of hysterical giggling from inside the bathroom.

Mr. Romney pulled open the door. The bathroom was huge. Watson was sitting on the closed toilet with Karen in his lap. David Michael, Jessi, and Mallory were cross-legged on the floor, howling with laughter.

Andrew and Isabella were in the bathtub. Mrs. Romney and Mrs. Brewer were busily stuffing pillows, cloth diapers, and fluffy towels all around them.

"Here are two more pillows," said Mr. Romney. "I opened up a couple of windows."

"Why did you do that?" I asked.

"To equalize the air pressure inside and out," Mrs. Romney replied.

"Weeeeeee!" Andrew squealed, tossing a rubber ducky in the air.

"Geeee!" burbled Isabella, who was strapped into a small baby seat.

"What is going on here?" I asked.

"Since we don't have a basement, the bathroom's the safest place in the house," Mr. Romney explained. "The metal plumbing strengthens the walls. The tub and the pillows protect the young ones."

RRRRRRRRRRMMMMMMMM!

David Michael stopped laughing. His face paled. "That's the tornado?"

Mr. Romney nodded gravely.

"Tornadoes can pick up cars and animals and sometimes houses," Karen announced. "They can blow a piece of straw clear through the trunk of a tree, like an arrow."

"Is that true?" David Michael asked.

"Well . . ." Mr. Romney sighed uneasily. "Yes. More or less. If it's severe."

No one was laughing anymore.

David Michael's eyes were watering. "Mommy?" he said in a tiny, fragile voice.

Mrs. Brewer sat next to him and he slipped into her lap.

Mr. Romney flicked on the radio.

". . . Cool, springlike air has combined with high winds to create the updrafts," crackled an announcer's voice. "We have several unconfirmed funnel sightings, and one F One twister has been confirmed. If you are outside in the affected area, head indoors or to the nearest hidey-hole —"

"Hidey-hole?" Watson said.

"Underground shelter," Mr. Romney explained.

"What do we do now?" Jessi asked.

Mr. and Mrs. Romney exchanged a glance.

"Nothing much we can do," Mrs. Romney replied softly, her hand holding Isabella's seat. "Nothing except sit tight and hope."

Claudia

Sunday

It is nitime. We are in the midle of the Bad Lands. Siting in a RV. Alone. Well, exept for a howling cyoty or two. And other weerd noises. Im sure their are snakes and ghealer monsters around, but I cant see.

Mr. Shafer has disapeerd. He shoud have been back by now.

It is becoming colder. Im shivering. Kristy and Stacy and Jeff are sleping, I dont know how they can do it.

If we dont make it and sombody finds this jurnal, plese contact the folowing pepole:

Mr. John & Mrs. Rioko Kishi, 58 Bradford Ct., Stoneybrook, CT...

"**W**hat are you writing?" Mary Anne whispered.

I flicked off my flashlight. "Nothing. Just the journal."

OOOOOOOOOOOOOOOOOOOO! howled the coyote.

"He's coming closer," I said.

"If we feed him, do you think he'll quiet down?" asked Dawn.

I gulped. *"Feed him?* Who's going to be first course?"

"I think coyotes are vegetarians," Dawn remarked.

"Too bad we didn't bring some seitan in a doggy bag from the Mall of America," I said.

"Claudia, will you *please* be quiet?" Stacey groaned from her bunk.

I gritted my teeth.

Those were the first words Stacey had said to me all day.

Our lives were in danger. We might be attacked by a pack of nonvegetarian wolves any minute. More than ever in our lives, we needed to band together. And all Stacey could do was scold me about interrupting her beauty sleep?

Grrrr. I was not going to give her the dignity of an answer.

For about the millionth time, I looked out the

window in the direction Mr. Schafer had gone. In the dim light of a nearly full moon, I could make out the dark ribbon of road that wound between the surrounding rocks.

"I wish it were pitch-black out there," I remarked. "The moonlight makes all these crater things look alive."

"Maybe we slipped into a time warp," Dawn said, "and we're back in the prehistoric days. Maybe that's why Dad can't find us. He went into the present or something. . . ."

"Dad?" called Jeff groggily.

"Sssshhh," Dawn said. "Go back to sleep."

Jeff sat bolt upright. "It's *not* a dream, is it?"

"SSSSSHHHH!" Dawn repeated.

"Why are you shushing? Nobody can hear us!" I said.

"Listen!" Dawn insisted.

I shut my mouth. In the distance I heard a faint hissing noise. Rattlesnake, I figured. Terrific. Just what we needed.

But as the sound grew louder, it became much more familiar.

"Is that a car?" That was Kristy, finally stirring from her sleep.

It *was* a car. I could see it now, headlight beams cutting through the darkness, vanishing and reappearing around the rock formations.

"He did it!" I shouted, pushing the door open.

"Claudia, shut it!" Kristy said. "You don't know that's him!"

RRRRRRRRRRRR!

The siren nearly made me jump through the roof.

A police car pulled up alongside the RV. The rear door flew open.

"Anybody home?" a familiar voice called out.

"Dad!" Dawn and Jeff screamed. They were out the RV door in a second.

Now Stacey was finally awake. We all stepped out of the RV, hugging ourselves against the cold.

Mr. Schafer must have asked, "Are you okay?" about a hundred times. He was trying not to look worried, but even in the dark I could see he was.

Boy, were we relieved. We could not stop chattering and asking questions. As we talked, two police officers went around to the trunk of their squad car, pulled out huge plastic containers of gasoline, and began filling the RV gas tanks.

"Sorry that took so long," Mr. Schafer said. "We lost our way there, and then all the stations were closed, and we had to find — oh, never mind. I'll tell you all about it in the next town. I'm taking everybody out for a late dinner!"

"Yyyyyyesss!" Jeff shouted. "I'm starving!"

The officers guided us through miles and miles of badlands. We finally arrived at a town called Wall.

As we cruised down Main Street, we passed a long, flat building with signs that read WALL DRUG STORE/CAFE/SHOPS. Farther on I spotted a couple of antique stores and art galleries. All of them were closed, but the police led us to a family restaurant that was still serving.

I have never eaten so well in my life. But I knew exactly where we had to go the next morning.

Guess what? The Wall Drug Store is world-famous. And it should be. It's sort of a cool, old-fashioned Wild West mall, without chain stores. We ate a fabulous breakfast there and browsed afterward.

But the place I liked best was an antique shop up the road. I wandered over there by myself and found a collection of dusty old paintings in the back.

Some of them were ugly — horses painted on velvet and stuff like that. But other paintings were much nicer, and I came across a few exquisite charcoal sketches.

I almost passed up the best one because someone had put it in a horrible, fancy gold frame.

But the sketch caught my eye. It was a skull with horns, a bull or longhorn or antelope. Whoever drew it must have been a fan of one of my favorite artists, Georgia O'Keeffe. Her paintings of skulls are famous. The pencil strokes, the angles, the perspectives were very much like hers. I've tried to imitate them, too, but this artist had done a better job. It wasn't the real thing, but I liked it. Despite the frame.

"How much is this?" I asked the owner.

He gave a quick glance and said, "I'll let you have it for two bucks. Frame's pretty valuable."

I dug my hands into my pockets and came up with a dollar and some change. "Maybe I can take it without the frame?" I suggested.

The owner smiled. "Aw, I wouldn't do that to you. Just give me one dollar. It's been sitting around here forever. It might as well find a home."

"Thanks!" I gave him the dollar and carried my new treasure outside. I looked around for a Dumpster or something, where I could ditch the frame.

"There you are!" Stacey was halfway down the block, marching toward me with a big scowl. "We have been looking all over for you!

129

We're supposed to go to that mammoth bone place. I knew you'd be out here collecting junk!"

"It's not —"

"Will you come on now, before Mr. Schafer has a heart attack?" Stacey spun around and stalked away, toward the Wall Drug Store. Looking back over her shoulder, she said, "And don't think you're going to fit that hideous monstrosity in the RV, either!"

I nearly threw it at her.

CHAPTER 13

Jessi

Sunday

I never thought
I'd be writing
in this journal
while sitting on
the floor of a
bathroom in Lester,
Oklahoma.
Outside, the twister
is howling. Inside,
Isabella and Andrew
are howling. The
rest of us are
trying to make
the best of it.
But it isn't easy....

"There she is! The Wicked Witch!" David Michael exclaimed, pointing toward the frosted bathroom window. "She flew by on her broom!"

Andrew looked horrified. "She did?"

"Yup. And a cow and a house and a white RV and —"

"Da-a-a-ad!" Andrew pushed away pillows and tried to climb out of the bathtub.

"David Michael, you're scaring your brother!" Mrs. Brewer scolded.

"I was just trying to cheer him up —"

The room suddenly shuddered. We all fell silent.

I heard a thump and a crash upstairs.

Mr. Romney cringed. "I didn't like that lamp anyway."

CRRRRACK!

That was from outside. Isabella started screaming. I grabbed Abby's hand on my right, Mallory's on my left. The wind seemed to be pounding on the bathroom walls.

"Are we going to be lifted into the air?" Karen asked.

"No," said Mr. Romney's voice. (*I hope not*, said his face.)

I thought of all the tornado damage I'd seen on news reports. The flattened homes, the tossed cars, the desperate people. The images had always seemed so far away. I wondered if my family was watching the news right now, knowing I was here, worrying, wondering. . . .

What a way to go. In a twister. After all those generations. Surviving the plantation. Moving North . . .

"Jessi?" Abby said. "Could you stop squeezing so hard?"

I loosened my grip. Abby and I exchanged a tense smile.

That was when I began hearing the rain. It was batting loudly against the house.

But the freight train noise was becoming softer. And the wind was no longer screeching.

"We have reports of property damage in Lester," droned the radio, "where one funnel has taken a sudden easterly course toward Buckland. . . ."

"East?" David Michael blanched. "Isn't that where Stoneybrook is?"

"Ssshhh!" Watson put his finger to his mouth, listening intently.

". . . still working to confirm other sightings. Conditions remain highly unstable. Stay indoors and listen to this station for further information."

We had to stay in the bathroom another half hour or so before we could leave.

When the tornado warning was finally lifted,

Jessi

Mr. Romney raced out of the bathroom. Abby, Mallory, David Michael, Karen, and I followed him through the house and out the front door.

"Oh my lord . . ." Abby said with a gasp.

At the end of the block, draped over a tree, was a roof.

Yes, a roof. Or at least the shingles from it, still stuck together but now twisted by the tree branches.

Next door, a smaller tree had toppled onto the lawn. "That was the cracking noise, huh?" I said.

Mr. Romney nodded. "Thank goodness it was only an F One."

"What does that mean?" Karen asked.

"That's one on a scale of zero to five," Mr. Romney explained. "*One* is classified as weak."

"That was *weak*?" Mallory said. "What's F Five like?"

Mr. Romney chuckled. "You don't want to know."

We had no more twisters that afternoon. But we could not stop talking about them. All through our ice-cream sundae dessert, Karen kept thinking she saw funnel clouds outside.

We were in a great mood as we left. Practically silly with relief.

"'Bye!" we all yelled.

"Gaaaaaah," said Isabella.

"We'll miss you, Isabella!" Mallory cried.

"Thank you, buddy," Watson said.

"Don't be strangers," Mr. Romney replied. "And don't worry, Ten Gallon is just outside Tornado Alley!"

Tornado Alley, by the way, is the region where twisters are most likely to hit. Ten Gallon, Texas, was our next stop. The home of the Walkin' Tall Rodeo.

The moment we took off, David Michael was chattering about it nonstop. "When they pick a kid out of the stands, I'm going to jump on that bronco!" he declared. "Yippee-ai-o-ki-ay!"

"How do you know they will pick a kid from the stands?" Karen asked.

David Michael ignored the question. "Ride 'em, cowboy! Pow! Pow!"

We were all exhausted when we pulled into an RV park just outside Ten Gallon, but David Michael didn't fall asleep until after midnight.

We were awakened by a "YAHOOOOO!" the next morning (courtesy of you-know-who).

"It is not 'yahoo,' David Michael," Karen grumbled. "Out West they say 'yee-hah.'"

"YEEEEE-HAAHHHHH!"

After breakfast in a local diner, we headed straight for the rodeo.

We had to park at least a quarter mile away.

Vendors were selling ten-gallon hats by the side of the road, and of course, we each bought one. David Michael yahooed and yee-hahed and yippeed his way to the gate.

Outside the rodeo was a kind of midway, full of Wild West–themed booths and a mechanical horse. But we went past it and into the stands.

We found some sitting space near the top. As we settled in, an older man next to us nudged his family over a bit.

"Thanks," Watson said.

"This is my first rodeo!" David Michael exclaimed. "Yee-hah! Where are the broncos and bulls?"

The old man chuckled and pointed across the ring. "Calf roping's the first event. See the calf in that chute?"

The "chute" was more like a tiny cage. Inside it was a cute little brown-and-white calf. It was mooing pathetically and looking very nervous. Nearby, in a gated wooden pen, a man in cowboy garb was saddling up a horse.

"What happens to the calf?" David Michael asked.

"Well, it runs out, all excited," the man said. "The cowboy lassoes it around the neck, then swings the rope around its legs to trip it up. *Whomp!* Down it goes. The horse knows to keep the rope tight, so the calf won't get away. Then the cowboy jumps off and has to grab the calf with both hands — one by the skin near its hind legs, the other by its neck. He lifts the calf, then, *whomp*, flips it to the ground again. Then he ties three of its legs together so it can't move. See? Whoever does it fastest wins!"

David Michael's smile had disappeared.

I was feeling a little queasy.

My heart went out to that poor little animal. This was not my idea of a fun public event. Ballet is more my speed.

"Do they kill the calf?" David Michael asked.

The old man chuckled. "Not supposed to. Just rough him up a bit. It's a rodeo, son."

David Michael stared at the calf silently for a moment. Then he turned toward Mrs. Brewer. "Mom? I don't feel so good."

Zoom. Off went Mrs. Brewer and David Michael.

Karen stood up. "I'm thirsty. I'll go with them."

"Me, too," added Abby, Mallory, Andrew, and me.

"I suppose I'll join you," Watson added.

The old man shouted, "I'll save your seats!"

We were already moving.

"That poor baby calf," I heard Karen say to Watson.

When we reached the midway, David Michael

immediately blurted out, "I want to ride the ponies!"

"I thought you were sick," Mrs. Brewer said.

"Well, um, I'm feeling a little better now," David Michael said.

"Okay, folks, lllet's ro-o-odeo!" a voice blared over a speaker.

A huge cheer went up.

"It's starting," Watson remarked. "Who wants to go back in?"

You know what? David Michael did not want to stop riding the mechanical horse. Mallory, Abby, and I practically had the midway games to ourselves. And Watson and Mrs. Brewer treated us to a big picnic of hot dogs and hamburgers.

Well, we did go to a rodeo. And we did have fun. Even though no one ever did ask to go back in.

Maybe next trip.

CHAPTER 14

Jeff

Tuesday

So far, I liked this trip. Getting lost was cool. The mammoth dig site was awesome. Now we're in Yellow Stone Park.

Guess what? There is NO ROCK CLIMBING here. The rock is too crumbly. That stinks, big time.

I'm trying to talk Dad into taking us to the Grand Teeton Mountains. There you can take rock climbing lessens. WAY COOL!

Anyway, Yellowstone
has guysers. If you step
on one and it irupts, it can
KILL YOU! Maybe I can
trick Dawn into going
across one.

JUST KIDDING!!!!!
Don't have a cow when
you read this, Dawn....

"Don't push," said my sister, Dawn.

"I'm not pushing," I replied.

"*Jeffrey!*" my dad scolded.

Dad always believes Dawn. That makes me so angry.

I wasn't doing anything. I mean, we were on these really narrow boardwalks and Dawn was walking really slowly. Way too slowly. I was behind her, and I was practically falling asleep. So I had to walk past her. I just brushed against her, that's all. Then she yelled at me, and Dad believed her.

Is that fair?

Girls are weird. Well, some girls. Definitely my sister. Claudia and Stacey, too. They're enemies now just because Claudia read some of Stacey's dumb journal. I mean, what's the point of keeping a journal if no one can read it? Mary Anne's another strange one. She used to be friendly, but not anymore. Dad thinks she's still mad at him for running out of gas in South Dakota. Kristy's okay, though. She likes to play ball.

Kristy also likes to walk fast on the boardwalks, like me. In Yellowstone, you have to use boardwalks. That's because geysers and mudpots are all around. Some of them look like normal dirt. Step on one and *fwooosh!* "Yeeaaaghhh!" Zapped with boiling hot water.

The biggest geyser? Old Faithful. They say it goes off every hour, but they're lying. It's more like an hour and ten minutes. Dawn says the delay is because of what people have done to the environment.

But that's what Dawn says about everything.

Okay, that's the boring stuff. Now for the BEST part of the trip.

Dad bought us sandwiches and we went for a hike in the woods. (That's not the best part yet.)

We found a place to eat near a big lake. (That's still not it.)

I brought my bathing suit, so I changed in the woods and went swimming. Everyone else came with me, but no one went in because they were too chicken. (Nope, not yet.)

Then we walked back to our picnic spot and guess what?

A bear was there. (Yup, that's it!)

He didn't see us. We slowly backed away, because that's what the guides tell you to do.

The other thing they tell you to do is tie your food up and hang it from a tree. We're no dummies. We had done that.

"Oh, no," Dawn said.

"Are we in danger?" Mary Anne asked.

I put my finger to my mouth without saying, "Ssssshhh." I mean, the bear could have heard us.

We watched him carefully. He was walking on all fours, just hanging out. When he was under our food, he looked up. His nose twitched. He reached with his hands a few times, but the food was way too high.

Then he plopped back down on all fours again — and walked right toward us!

"Whatever you do, don't run," Dad whispered.

The bear looked right into my eyes. I just stared him down.

Well, I'm pretty sure that's what happened. Actually, I'm not a hundred percent positive the bear even saw us. He took another look at the food. Then he just moseyed away.

You should have seen us. We looked like we were playing a game of freeze tag but no one was It.

About four hours later I finally breathed. Well, it seemed that long.

"Follow me," Dad said. "And be quiet."

We tiptoed back to our picnic spot. We took down the food, and Dad stuffed it into his backpack. He found a trail in the opposite direction from where the bear went.

Jeff

You never saw hikers move so fast. We were more like bikers.

When we got to the place where the RV was parked, we couldn't stop laughing. I don't know why. Even gloomy old Mary Anne was cracking up.

You know what else is cool about Yellowstone National Park? The canyon. (It's called the Grand Canyon, but it's not *the* Grand Canyon). Also the Upper Falls. The falls are three-hundred-feet high, which is like a twenty-story building.

We camped overnight in Yellowstone. I wanted to pitch a tent outdoors, but the girls were afraid of bears, so we slept inside.

The next morning I asked Dad if we could go to the Grand Tetons for rock climbing.

"Aren't you too young for it?" Dad asked. "Rock climbing is dangerous."

"It is?" Dawn said. "Then let him go."

Ha-ha. Sisters.

Well, we did go. And Dad signed me up for a lesson. My instructor's name was Peter Rogers. He asked if anyone else wanted to take a lesson.

"You wouldn't get me up there in a million years," said my sister.

Mary Anne and Stacey and Claudia backed away as if the rock were made of moldy cheese. Kristy was too tired.

144

"Guess it's just you and me," Mr. Rogers said.

He gave me a helmet and tied a rope between us, but guess what? You don't use the rope to climb. Just your feet and arms. You have to grab on to the tiniest handholds. The rope stays slack. It's there just in case of emergency. The guy on top anchors it onto a rock.

Guess what else? I, Jeff Schafer, reached the top! I'll bet no other ten-year-olds have done it, but I didn't ask.

Anyway, after we rested a minute, Mr. Rogers said, "Time to rappel!"

Yes! I'd been waiting for this. Rappelling is walking backward down a rock. It looks so cool on TV. Mr. Rogers wrapped the rope around me in something called a Prussik loop. He said if I fell, it would tighten and I'd hang under him.

Great.

Then he said I had to hold on to the rope, stand up, and lean back — on a rock that was almost straight up and down! I was so scared I nearly cried.

"I — I — I can't!" I shouted.

"Are you okay?" Dawn called from below.

Okay? I was about to die.

It took me soooo long. But I did it. I was standing *outward*, like someone walking on a wall. Then I started edging backward down the rock, letting a little rope out at a time.

Then walking.

Then bouncing.

"Wooooo! This is great!" I shouted. It was much easier than I'd thought!

You should have seen the girls' faces when I reached the bottom. They were so jealous.

Oh, well. They could have done it, too.

It was their choice.

CHAPTER 15

Mallory
☺

Wednesday

What a trip! We survived the twister and the rodeo. We even survived a close encounter with...

Liz Hoyer!

I could not believe it. There was her car, with the same dent on the front bumper, in the parking lot of a rest stop in Albuquerque, New Mexico. Clear across the country from Chincoteague!

The Hoyers were happy to see us. We told them all about our trip since we last met.

Liz laughed about our reaction to the rodeo. She said we were "such typical Easterners." (Guess where she comes from? Rhode Island. Guess how many rodeos she's been to? Zero.)

That's Liz.

Anyway, onward to Four Corners...

"Zuni . . ." Watson murmured. "Hmmm, why is that name familiar?"

I stopped writing. "*Zuni? Where?*"

"On that road sign we just passed," Watson answered.

Jessi sat forward excitedly. "Of course! We're in New Mexico!"

"Wasn't that the Pens Across America town?" Mrs. Brewer asked.

"Yes!" I replied.

"Well, it's the next turnoff," Watson said. "Thirtysomething miles, I think."

I should explain. Zuni is the name of a Native American tribe. It's also the name of their reservation and the town they live in. The kids in Stoneybrook Elementary School had become pen pals with Zuni kids in a program called Pens Across America. (Six of my brothers and sisters were involved.) When the Zuni elementary school burned to the ground, Dawn organized a fund-raising drive. The Stoneybrook kids sent supplies, clothing, and donations to help out.

The Zunis were able to build a new school. I don't know how much of a role our donations played, but the Zuni elementary school principal wrote to thank us. He said we were a big help.

"Wouldn't it be fun to see their reservation?" Jessi said.

"Their new school?" I added.

"Their sheep?" David Michael said.

Abby cracked up. "*Sheep?*"

"My pen pal, Sam Wright? His family herds them," David Michael explained.

"Well, we are running a bit behind schedule. . . ." Watson said, glancing at his watch.

"Pleeeeease?" David Michael said. "Can't we skip dumb old Four Corners?"

"Hey!" Karen protested. (She, by the way, had not been in Pens Across America. Her school, Stoneybrook Academy, was not involved.)

Another sign for Zuni was coming up. Watson looked at Mrs. Brewer.

"Who knows when they'll ever have this opportunity again?" she said with a smile.

"If Dawn knew we were in this area and didn't visit Zuni, she'd never forgive us," I remarked.

"All right," Watson said, "but let's make it brief."

"YEEEEE-HAAAAHHH!" whooped David Michael.

The Zuni exit is in the town of Gallup, New Mexico. We turned off, heading south onto a narrower highway.

I love the scenery of the Southwest. It's so . . . red. That's because of the clay in the soil. All around you, these long, flat stretches of land rise up out of the desert. They're called mesas, and they look like tables made of sand and rock. It's as if giants set up for a big convention, then decided to leave.

About an hour from Gallup we saw the first sign of life. It was a herd of sheep walking across the highway, led by a boy and an older man.

They appeared to be heading for the Zuni reservation, which was tucked in among the mesas. Some of the pen pals had sent photos, so I recognized it immediately.

"Okay, tell me where to stop," Watson said, driving onto a local road.

"Let's ask someone where the school is," Mrs. Brewer suggested.

That wasn't going to be easy. It seemed as if everyone was inside.

We wound around for awhile and finally ended up at a big plaza. It was surrounded by typical Zuni houses that look like little mesas themselves. They are one story high and flat-roofed. Some were made of stone but others of adobe brick, the same color as the soil.

People were walking across the plaza, carrying groceries or tools. Kids were chasing after one another.

Mallory

"This is where they have that new year festival!" David Michael exclaimed.

"Sha'la'ko," I said. The Zuni kids had told us all about their huge celebration. It takes a year to prepare for it. At the beginning of December, masked dancers in elaborate costumes dance for three days, sometimes for ten hours straight. Zunis usually welcome visitors, but no outsiders are allowed to attend Sha'la'ko.

We were attracting a lot of blank stares. None of the conversations that we heard through the open window were in English, but Watson climbed out and asked around anyway. He was smiling when he came back. "The last fellow I talked to? His daughter was in the Pens Across America program. The last name is Green. He seemed very excited. And now I have directions."

"Rats," David Michael said. "That wasn't my pen pal."

"Green . . ." I said. The name did sound familiar.

We were in front of the school in minutes. It was flat like the adobe houses but long and modern looking, with tinted windows and a huge playing field.

We climbed out and walked toward the building. I spotted a bronze plaque beside the front doors. I moved closer to read it:

THE GENEROUS CONTRIBUTIONS
OF THE FOLLOWING INDIVIDUALS
AND ORGANIZATIONS
HELPED IN THE SPEEDY REBUILDING OF OUR SCHOOL
AFTER A DEVASTATING FIRE.
WE HOLD THEM IN OUR HEARTS AND OUR MEMORIES.

Underneath was a list. I gasped when I read the first name:

THE CHILDREN OF STONEYBROOK, CONNECTICUT

"That's us!" David Michael cried out.

"Dawn would be so proud," Jessi remarked.

"Did we spell it right?"

We all turned toward the voice. A short, dark-haired man with sunglasses was climbing out of a car. As he walked toward us, he was beaming. "Joseph Woodward. I'm the principal. Mr. Green called to tell me we had visitors from our favorite Eastern town."

"You wrote a letter to us!" I said.

"You bet!"

As Mr. Woodward shook our hands, Karen piped up. "You spelled Stoneybrook right. But it was not *all* the children. Just one particular school."

Mr. Woodward smiled. "When you're given a beautiful mosaic, you appreciate all the stones,

153

not just the mother-of-pearl. Your entire town is precious to us."

That was nice. It even made Karen smile.

Mr. Woodward showed us around the school. By the time we were through, a small crowd had formed out front — including Sam Wright, David Michael's pen pal.

What did they talk about? Sha'la'ko? The great fire? The differences in Zuni and Stoneybrook lifestyles?

No. Computer games. (Figures.)

We also met Nancy Green (who was Haley Braddock's pen pal), Conrad White and Rachel Redriver (my brother Adam's and my sister Margo's pen pals), and a few others. Some of them gave us notes to take home.

Then the Greens invited us all to their house for lunch — and the entire crowd came!

I thought Watson would be nervous about how much time we were spending there. But he was having a blast.

Sometimes last-minute plans are the best.

CHAPTER 16

Dawn

Wednesday

Well, we just entered Idaho. Soon we'll cross over to Oregon, then on to Seattle, Washington. We have not found what I wanted. No ghost towns left, I guess. At least not in the North.

That's okay. I can't complain. I've been reading about an Oregon company that makes wonderful soybean-based products. They offer free samples on their tour. That might be fun....

Dawn

"Soybean-based products?" Kristy said.

"That's lame, Dawn," Jeff remarked.

"Isn't there a major ice-cream company based in Oregon?" Claudia asked.

"Well, *I* like the idea," I protested.

The truth? I wasn't thrilled about my idea, either. But I was desperate. Claudia, Mary Anne, and Jeff had been to their destinations. Kristy had been to several. Stacey was about to go to hers. I needed one, too. Something out of the ordinary. Something unpredictable. Something that said *Dawn*.

Not, however, something impossible. A ghost town? What had I been thinking?

Sigh. Our RV now had an official case of Advanced Grumps. Not only Stacey and Claudia and Mary Anne. Me, too.

I stared grumpily out the window as we pulled into a rest stop.

"All ashore that's going ashore," Dad shouted. "I'll fill up."

We had pulled into just about every single rest stop since South Dakota. I know Dad was determined not to run out of gas again, but this was ridiculous.

Grump, grump, grump.

Claudia and Mary Anne decided to go inside.

156

I grumped along behind them. I glanced at the brochures in a rack near the wall.

National parks, state parks — been there.

Art museum — done that.

Idaho Shakespeare Festival, Zoo Boise . . . My eyes scanned the dozens of offers.

"Find anything?" Mary Anne asked, walking back from the women's room.

"What a waste of paper," I muttered. "All those dead trees."

"People want to know about these places, Dawn," Mary Anne said gently.

"Why not collect them all in one brochure? Or have a computer screen? Is it really necessary to have a stack of brochures for an electricity museum? Old Idaho Penitentiary? The Buzzard Gulch tour —"

The words caught in my throat. I stared at that last brochure.

"Want anything?" called Claudia's voice from the direction of the vending machines.

"Listen to this!" I pulled out the brochure and read it aloud. "'Buzzard Gulch — Idaho's Turn-of-the-Century Haunted Village, Lovingly Re-Created for Today's Visitor.'"

"I meant candy!" Claudia shouted.

I ignored her and kept on reading: "'Buzzard Gulch sprang up in 1899 when Junius Phelps discovered gold along the Black River. It prospered until June 1902, when the town records abruptly stop. In July, Phelps's brother came to visit. He was unable to find anyone — every single person had disappeared. The only signs of life were the buzzards.'"

"Ew," Mary Anne said.

"This is it!" I shouted.

"Whuh izzh ick?" asked Claudia, who now had a mouthful of Milky Way bar.

"We are on our way to a real, live ghost town!"

To drive to Buzzard Gulch, we had to take a narrow blacktop road. The turnoff was marked by a big poster of a bearded ghost wearing Western gear.

"Cool," Jeff said.

Dad looked worried. "I hope it's not too far off the beaten track."

"We just filled up, Dad," I reminded him.

A mile or so down the road was a billboard for the Buzzard Gulch Motel and Time-Share Condos.

Soon after, we saw one for Ol' Junius's Gen'ral Store.

And the Ghost of a Chance Saloon and Family Restaurant.

And the Wild West Souvenir Shoppe/Fax Centre.

"I think the track has been beaten," Stacey remarked.

Finally we came to a parking lot. At the other end of it was a big wooden gate decorated with fake cobwebs and a sign with jagged letters that read GO BACK BEFORE IT'S TOO LATE! A man wearing a Hawaiian shirt was standing next to it, grinning, while his wife took a photo.

Beyond the gate was a long dirt street, lined with ruined old shacks.

Very sturdy-looking ruined old shacks. Like a movie set.

"BOOOO-AHHH-HA-HA-HA-HA!" blared a voice from a speaker in the trees.

"Puh-leeze," Stacey remarked.

This was not what I was expecting. Not at all. I wanted real abandoned buildings. Not a theme park. Not Buzzard Gulch Tourist Trap.

Everyone was staring at me.

Tears welled up in my eyes. This trip was jinxed. I felt humiliated. I wanted to run back to the RV. We could still go to the soybean-products factory. Anything would be better than this.

"Let's go-o-o-o-o!" Jeff cried, racing toward the gate.

Dad ran after him, camera poised.

"Wait!" I cried out.

Too late.

I couldn't look my friends in the eye. "Sorry, guys," I said. "I thought —"

Claudia was already on her way. "Come on!"

"Good choice, Dawn," Mary Anne said, following behind her.

Stacey giggled. "Ethan will die when I tell him about this."

Huh?

They were being kind. That had to be it.

I slumped along behind them.

We all walked toward the entrance. We bought tickets at a booth marked ADMISSION FOR PROSPECTIN'. The ticket taker was dressed in a nineteenth-century costume. "Proceed at your own risk," she said.

Right.

"Stop, thief!" a shout rang out.

POW! POW!

Two men with handlebar mustaches were running down the unpaved street toward us. The first one was wearing raggedy clothes and carrying a big burlap sack. He was being chased by a man wearing a fringed leather vest and brandishing a silver revolver.

"Catch that varmint!" the second man shouted.

The crowd of tourists stood and watched. The first man eyed us all, then ran straight toward

160

me. "'Scuse me, ma'am. Hold this while I search for some refreshment."

He gave the bag to me. Then he ran through the crowd and into a building marked TAVERN.

My friends were cracking up. Jeff, across the street with Dad, was doubled over with laughter.

The bag was huge but really light. It must have been stuffed with Styrofoam. Now the man with the revolver ran to me, glowering.

"Ma'am, gimme back my fertilizer!" he growled.

The crowd roared.

I threw the bag back to him. I was so embarrassed.

Well, you can imagine what the rest of the visit was like. A square-dance band appeared in the middle of the street and some old guy with a potbelly started dancing with Claudia.

Another guy with blacked-out teeth ran down the street with a sifter full of fake gold, shouting, "I'm rich! I'm rich!" only to fall on his face and send the trinkets flying into the crowd.

Inside the "Phelps family ghost house" was a holograph of the Phelps family at dinner, each of the members glaring at us as if we had intruded on their privacy.

Next was the film *Story of Buzzard Gulch* in the Burlesque Theater. It explained that Buzzard

Gulch was an actual place, but the ruins were "carefully developed for today's entertainment needs by the country's leading theme park engineers."

"This is s-o-o-o-o-o corny," Stacey whispered to me at one point.

I agreed. But you know what? As we all descended into the pitch-blackness of the Underground Gold Mine Log Flume, I realized something.

I was having a great time.

The soybean products could wait.

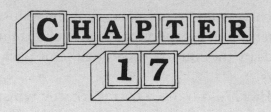

CHAPTER 17

KAREN

THURSDAY

DAVID MICHAEL SAID WE SHOULD SKIP FOUR CORNERS.
I ASKED HIM WHY. HE SHOWED ME A MAP. HE POINTED TO
WHERE *NEW* MEXICO, ARIZONA, COLORADO, AND UTAH
MEET. EACH STATE WAS A DIFFERENT COLOR. HE SAID THE
STATES ARE NOT REALLY DIFFERENT COLORS. HE SAID THEY DO
NOT HAVE LINES BETWEEN THEM. SO THE FOUR CORNERS
WILL JUST BE A PATCH OF DIRT.

THEN HE TOLD ME I SHOULD WANT TO GO TO A DINOSAUR
SITE. I TOLD HIM THAT WAS A PATCH OF DIRT, TOO. I WAS JUST
JOKING. BUT NOW HE IS MAD AT ME.

BOO AND BULL FROGS.

"But what are we going to do when we're there?" asked David Michael.

"I am going to put my left foot in Arizona," I began, "and my right foot in New Mexico. Then I am going to lean down. I will put my left hand in Utah and my right hand in Colorado. I will be in four states at the same time. And I will look northeast. That's where Stoneybrook is. Then I —"

"But you won't see Stoneybrook," David Michael interrupted. "It's too far away."

"I *know* that. It's just for fun. You see, when I am in all four states, I will look toward Stoneybrook and wave to my friends back home."

"Then you won't be in four states anymore!" David Michael exclaimed.

"Why?"

"Because one hand will be waving."

David Michael was laughing. He was right. But I did not think he was funny at all.

I looked at the mesas outside.

I thought of our stop with the Zuni people. That was gigundoly fun. We had dinner with the elementary school principal and his wife. She's a teacher. She could not eat everything we ate because she has diabetes. She said many Zuni people have that. I told Mrs. Woodward about Stacey. When the Woodwards visit Stoneybrook, I will introduce them.

As soon as we left the Zuni reservation, Daddy and Elizabeth began arguing. I could not hear what they were saying, but they both looked at their watches a lot.

"Karen, sweetheart," Daddy finally said, "we are running late. Our trip to Zuni took a long time. We had not planned on that. We still have to go to the Grand Canyon, the San Diego Zoo, and Palo City. They are all due west. If we drive straight to the Grand Canyon, we will be there before nightfall."

I had followed our whole trip on a map. I knew the Four Corners was not due west. It was north. "But the Four Corners was where I wanted to go," I said.

"We know, Karen," Elizabeth replied. "We wondered if you'd prefer the Petrified Forest and Painted Desert. Those are west, too."

"Yeeaaaa!" David Michael said. "I want to see them!"

"How did the desert get painted?" asked my brother, Andrew.

"With sagebrushes!" David Michael answered. He started cracking up.

I was not listening. I was thinking about what Elizabeth said. Those things sounded pretty good.

But they were not the Four Corners. That is the only place in the whole country where four states touch. If we did not go, I might never see it again.

A tear fell into my lap. I did not even know I was crying.

Jessi did. "You really don't want to do that, huh?" she said.

"We could skip the Grand Canyon," Abby suggested, "and go straight from the Four Corners to San Diego."

Abby did not want to go to the Grand Canyon. I could tell.

Elizabeth turned around. I tried to wipe away my tears, but she saw me.

She made a sad face and gave me a tissue. Then she whispered something to Daddy.

Daddy nodded and took a deep breath. "We can do both," he said. "It's all right."

I knew he would say that. My daddy is great.

Guess what? We did see something gigundoly fantastic on the way to Four Corners. It's called Ship Rock Pinnacle. The Navajo word for it is *tse be dahi*. That means "rock with wings." You can see it from a hundred miles away, and it looks like the skyline of a whole city.

Guess what else? I, Karen Brewer, stood in four states *and* waved to Stoneybrook!

167

The place where the states meet is marked. A monument is near it. Lots of tourists were doing just what I wanted to do. Boy, was David Michael surprised. He thought we would never find the exact spot.

Guess what else *else*? David Michael wanted to step in all four states even more than I did!

All of us did it. Foot, foot, hand, hand. Just the way I described.

Then I thought of a better way. I stood right *on* the spot. I let parts of my feet be in each state.

That was how I could wave.

David Michael said that was cheating, but he is wrong.

"Grand Canyon, ho!" Daddy said when we were finished.

We drove west. And you would not believe the place we passed through.

It is called Monument Valley. The rock formations were gigundo gigundo! Kind of scary, too. We stopped to look, and no one could speak for a long time.

I read that the Native Americans called Monument Valley a sacred place. I am not surprised.

We could not stay long. It was almost dark, and we had to go.

Do you know what time we arrived at the Grand Canyon? I don't. I was asleep. Daddy only said it was "the wee hours of the morning."

He woke me up, but just to say good night and tuck me in.

"I am sorry I made you drive so far," I said.

Daddy smiled. "I wouldn't have missed it."

I knew he would say that.

I was having such a great time.

GAS FOOD LODGING

CHAPTER 18

Stacey

                   Thursday

We made it!

I ♥♥♥♥ Seattle!!! It is WAY COOL!

Move over, Big Apple! (Just kidding.)

It's so great to see a CITY again. Especially one as beautiful as this. Mountains on one side, a bay on the other.

We've arrived in plenty of time for the Seattle Mariners game, which makes Kristy happy. Jeff's dying to go to the Space Needle, which looks like a flying saucer on a radio tower. Mary Anne wants to ride the monorail. Dawn wants to check out the Pike Place Market. Mr. Schafer wants to shake Bill Gate's hand.

It is now 11:52. Which means one thing. Everything must wait. Our first stop is the Corner Coffee Shop!

Now, to find it. I know it's near some park....

"I see a Regrade Park," Kristy said, her face buried in a map, "a Steinbrueck Park, a Freeway Park, a Westlake Park, a Boren-Pike-Pine Park, a Pioneer Square Park, a City Hall Park, a Kobe Terrace Park, a Hing Hay Park. . . . Which one is it?"

"I *thought* I wrote it down!" I said for about the fiftieth time, flipping through the pages of my journal. "But all I see is 'near Third Avenue.' That's where he's staying."

"Third Avenue runs the whole length of downtown Seattle," Kristy said. "He didn't mention a cross street?"

"He didn't know," I replied. "He's not a native, Kristy."

"Cities have lots of parks," Claudia said. "It's a good idea to ask for names."

Uh-huh. Not a word to me through seven states, and this is what Claudia breaks her silence with? What nerve.

"Would you like to check?" I asked, holding out my journal. "You probably know it better than I do."

"Whaaaat?" Claudia said.

"Stacey, please," Mary Anne said gently.

"Can't we just skip the dumb coffee shop?" Jeff grumbled.

"To our right," Mr. Schafer said, "we are approaching beautiful Westlake Park."

I turned back to the window. Opposite the park was a mall, with tons of shops. Mr. Schafer was slowing down.

"The Starthrower Coffee Bar?" Mary Anne asked.

"No . . ." I was looking past the mall now, to the next block.

On the corner was a small, old-fashioned shop with a sign hanging above its front door. The sign was angled toward us, so I couldn't make out the words until we were closer . . .

Yes. *Yes!*

"The Corner Coffee Shop!" I shouted.

Claudia looked shocked. Dismayed. I gave her a quick Look, but I had more important things to think about.

My hair looked like a buzzard's nest. I was barefoot. I felt tired and exhausted.

Morph time.

I slipped my feet into my Doc Martens. I reached for the brush lying on my bunk and furiously pulled it through my hair.

As I straightened out my clothes, Mr. Schafer came to a stop by a parking meter.

This was it. My heart was pounding.

Ethan was in there. I could just picture him. Like a scene in a movie. He's looking at his watch. At his menu. At the window. Wondering, worrying.

Then . . . he sees a flash of blonde hair by the door. The café falls silent. His inner torment melts away. Two words are on his mind, words locked inside him, waiting to burst loose. *She's here.* He rises as she floats toward him on a gust of pure joy. . . .

Oh, this was so romantic, I wanted to scream!

"Stacey?" Kristy said. "You have a Chunky wrapper on your butt."

"Oh! Thanks!" I quickly brushed it off. "So. Um, I'll meet you here after the game?"

"I'll go in with you," Mr. Schafer suggested, "in case he's not there."

"Let's all go!" Jeff said.

Yikes!

A flash of blonde hair, a dad, four tired girls, and a ten-year-old? *Not* in the script.

"No!" I blurted out. "I'll, uh, just wave to you through the window when I see him."

"Fair enough," Mr. Schafer replied.

I pulled myself together and swept out of the RV, to a chorus of "Good luck"s. (No, there was no "good luck" from Claudia.)

I walked across the street and into the coffee shop. Not too quickly. Not too eagerly. *Always leave them wanting more.* I don't know who said that. Somebody famous.

I stopped inside the door and tossed back my hair.

No one seemed to notice.

I gazed around the tables. A family of four. A couple in their twenties. Two nerdy-looking guys with laptops. A woman reading a newspaper and sipping coffee.

I checked my watch. Eleven fifty-eight. Maybe I was too early.

"May I help you?" a waiter asked.

"I'm meeting someone," I said. "A guy, black hair, about fifteen, earring in one ear?"

The waiter shook his head. "Nope."

I left the shop and went back to the sidewalk. "Not here yet!" I called out.

"I'll wait," Mr. Schafer shouted back.

I was sort of hoping he wouldn't say that. The RV was never beautiful to begin with. After one and a half weeks on the road, it looked as if it had been through a mud bath and a grime rinse. Very romantic.

Oh, well, maybe Ethan wouldn't notice the van.

I took a seat at a table in the back. A waiter asked to take my order, but I said, "I'm expecting one more."

Fifteen minutes later, I was still expecting.

By 12:25, I wasn't. I was in a blind panic.

Was I wrong about the time? The day? *What was going on here?*

Kristy, Claudia, Dawn, and Jeff were window-shopping at the mall. Mr. Schafer was standing outside the RV, trying to keep an eye on them while reading a newspaper.

I ran outside again. "It's been a half hour."

Mr. Schafer smiled wearily. "He's an artist, right? Aren't artists always late?"

"Maybe it's the wrong place!" I spotted a bank of pay phones at the corner. I had Ethan's phone number in my pocket. "Be right back!"

I sprinted to a phone and tapped out Ethan's number.

With each ring of the phone, I felt my insides jangle.

"Hello, you've reached 555-2876. We can't come to the phone, so please leave a message. . . ."

Booop!

"This is Ethan . . . I mean, Stacey! At the Corner. I'm Stacey, and can Ethan call me? No, he can't, what am I saying? McGill — Stacey McGill. Um . . . I'll call later."

Click.

Great. A message in Martian.

I tapped out the information number and reached an operator. "Seattle, please. I'm supposed to meet someone at the Corner Coffee Shop? But maybe it's not it? I mean, is there another place with the same name?"

"Corner, or Kona?" the operator asked.

Duh. *"Kona?"*

"Yes. I have a Corner Coffee Shop, a Corner Coffee Hut, a Corner Coffee House, and a Kona Coffee Shop."

"All of them!" I blurted out. "Just the addresses, okay?"

I fished around in my pockets for a pen. Nothing.

Good old Mr. Schafer. He'd crossed the street, and now he was digging out a pen and a folded-up sheet of paper.

I took down all the addresses. Politely, calmly, I thanked the operator.

I didn't scream until I hung up.

"It's too late now. We'll never find him!"

"Never say never!" Mr. Schafer said, then turned toward the others. "Come on, troops! We're moving out!"

Kristy sat in front with the map. I sat behind her with my sheet. We zipped through downtown Seattle.

The Corner Coffee Hut was by the Amtrak station. No Ethan.

The Corner Coffee House was near the aquarium. No luck there, either.

The Kona Coffee Shop was in a cool neighborhood near the Space Needle. Lots of people closer to our age. I had high hopes for this one.

Ethanless.

In the RV, Kristy was tapping on her watch. "Pregame festivities begin in five minutes."

"Stacey, are you *sure* you didn't write it down?" Mr. Schafer asked for the millionth time.

"I'll check again." I reached up for my pack.

No pack.

I glared at Claudia. "Has anyone seen my journal? It was in my pack."

"Why are you looking at me?" Claudia asked.

"Last time I saw your pack," Mary Anne said, "you were wearing it in the Corner Coffee Shop."

I smacked my forehead. "Oh, no! I left it there!"

Kristy turned pale. "Well, uh, maybe Mr. Schafer can drop us off at the Kingdome —"

"We're in this together," Mr. Schafer said, starting up the engine. "To the Corner Coffee . . . whatever."

I slumped into my seat as we sped away. I felt as if a drain cap had popped open in each of my toes. All at once, my life was seeping out.

"Stacey, he'll get your message," Mary Anne said.

"Sure," I grunted. "If he can decode it. If he

even wants to talk to me now. Maybe that wasn't his number. The answering machine message didn't give a name."

By the time we arrived at the Corner Coffee Shop, I felt like a puddle of split-pea soup. I oozed out the RV door and walked into the shop. My shoes were untied but I didn't feel like doing anything about it. As I opened the front door, I saw my reflection in the glass and wondered who had drawn the gray sacks under my eyes. Lovely.

I walked straight to the cashier. "Excuse me, but did you find a green backpack, with leather trim —?"

"Stacey?"

Gulp.

I could not have heard that. Another Stacey was in the shop. Another guy whose voice sounded like Ethan's.

"Stacey! It's Ethan! Behind you — by the window!"

Yikes.

No time to think. Lights, camera, action. The Meeting. Scene one, take two.

I smiled. I took my backpack from the cashier. I turned. I felt my untied shoelaces whip against my ankles.

Aauugh. I suddenly felt as if my feet were a size 400.

Ignore them. Don't look down.

I tossed my hair casually back. I waved. I stepped toward him.

Tip-tippety-tip, went my shoelaces.

"Coming through!"

A waiter zoomed by. I jumped away. I landed on a shoelace and stumbled against the wall.

Ethan was laughing. *Laughing!*

I was mortified.

I wanted to run outside. Hop back into the RV and head for the badlands.

Some romantic movie. This was a comedy!

Ethan rushed to me and took my hand. As we walked toward the table, he said, "Weak in the knees, huh?"

All my tension bubbled up. All the waiting and frantic phone calls and chasing around town. Who was I trying to kid? This was real life, and I was *mad*!

"Where were you?" I demanded.

Ethan shrugged. "Right here."

"But I waited until almost twelve-thirty!"

Ethan's face fell. "You didn't get my messages?"

"What messages?"

"That I had to change the time. I made sure to leave them on your mom's answering machine *and* your dad's. I figured you'd be talking to at least one of them —"

"Oh, Ethan," I said with a groan. "They're both on vacation!"

Ethan winced. "I'm sorry, Stacey. I didn't know."

"It's not your fault. I didn't tell you," I said with a sigh. Out of the corner of my eye, I saw the driver's door of the RV open up. "Uh, sit, okay? I'll be right back."

I darted outside. Mr. Schafer was stepping out onto the street. I waved him back. "He's here!"

Mr. Schafer grinned and reached for the door handle. "See you after the game!"

As I opened the door of the Corner Coffee Shop, I heard the RV roaring away.

Ethan was red-faced. "Stacey, I am such a dork —"

"No, I am," I said. "I had your number. I should have called to check in. And I'm sorry I yelled at you, Ethan. It's been kind of a long trip. Fun, but . . . I don't know. Tense, too. My best friend and I aren't even talking."

"With all those people? I'd be bouncing off the walls." Ethan suddenly laughed. "Did you really see a bear in Yellowstone?"

"You got that letter? That was so-o-o-o scary!"

"My favorite was the one about the badlands."

"A police escort! We had a police escort to the Wall Drug Store!"

Before long I was going through the trip, stop by stop. The Mall of America. Buzzard Gulch. The Rock and Roll Hall of Fame. The mammoth site. The Art Institute of Chicago.

Ethan hung on my every word. Half the time he was interrupting me to ask for details. Half the time we were howling. We sent the waiter away three times before we ordered anything. I'm surprised they didn't kick us out.

When I reached the story of my adventures in Seattle, we both were laughing so hard we nearly lost our sandwiches. I was practically crying.

"What a trip, Stacey," Ethan said. "You'll never forget it your whole life. I'm telling my parents to *drive* next time we come out here!"

I sat back and sipped my iced tea. All day I'd been so nervous, angry, tired, cramped, impatient. Now, at the Corner Coffee Shop, I felt as if I'd finally begun to unwind. All the memories of my trip were bubbling around inside. Funny, happy, tiring, scary memories. And I felt myself becoming strangely sad.

I'd been across the whole country. Coast to coast. Soon we'd be in California, and then home.

It had been a great trip.

I was already missing it.

"Want to take a walk?" Ethan asked.

"Mr. Schafer's picking me up here after the Mariners game," I said.

"They won't be here until at least five or five-fifteen. We have plenty of time."

We paid the bill and strolled toward the bay.

As we walked along the waterfront, Ethan told me about his art museum trip. He described a sculpture he was working on. He told me about his stepsister in college and his little brother. He listened to the long story of my life and laughed in all the right places.

I always knew Ethan was cool. I didn't know he was so sweet. And warm. And that his arm fit so perfectly around my shoulder. And that walking with him felt like gliding.

If he hadn't stopped at the Space Needle, I think we would have walked straight into Canada.

But we didn't. We took the elevator to the top. We stood squooshed together among the crowd, gazing down at the entire city. In the distance, broad, snowcapped Mount Rainier was watching over us like a guardian.

"Awesome," Ethan said.

"Yeah," I replied.

He smiled. I smiled back.

Soon I wasn't noticing the crowd at all. Or the view of the city. Or the mountain.

Just Ethan and me. And the feeling of our kiss.

Ethan was exactly right.

Awesome.

The RV did not show up at the Corner Coffee Shop until six. Which was fine by me. I didn't mind the extra time with Ethan.

It was rough saying good-bye. As we drove off, I knelt on Claudia's bed, which looked out a side window. Ethan and I waved to each other until he was out of sight.

I plopped onto the mattress just as Claudia came over to reach for some chips by the pillow.

"Oh," she said.

"Ohhhhh." I sighed. "Claudia, he is so-o-o perfect."

"Really?"

I gushed about the last few hours — every step, every feeling. As if reminding myself. Printing it in my memory.

Claudia sat beside me and listened to every word. She fed me chips. She asked questions. She cheered when I told her about the kiss.

Then, when I was done, she said, "Stacey? I'm confused."

"About what?" I said.

"Are we friends again?"

Whoa. I had completely forgotten about our fight.

My smile disappeared.

But you know what? I just did not feel like being mad. Not after today.

"Claudia," I began, "did you really read my journal?"

"No," Claudia replied.

I nodded. "Well, maybe I can read some of it to you. It's really fun."

Claudia burst out laughing.

I did, too.

Arguing is so dumb.

CHAPTER 19

Abby

Friday
PERSONAL JOURNAL

Mallory asked me
if I wanted to
write in the trip
journal. She
noticed I hadn't
done so for a while.
I said no.
What would I
have written?

"I've made it to the Grand Canyon. Finally"?

"I'm at the most amazing spot in America and I feel as if I'm going to throw up"?

Nahhh. Better not say anything at all.....

"Woww..."

"Who-o-oa..."

"Oh my lord..."

"Cooooool..."

Someone should do a study about what happens to people when they see the Grand Canyon.

I'll tell you one thing. Their vocabulary shrinks.

Why? It's simple. The Grand Canyon is the most amazing sight in the country. It's as if the earth yawned one morning and then kept opening up, practically to the center. Pictures, movies, videos — nothing compares to seeing the Grand Canyon in person. It staggers you.

I knew all that before I ever visited the canyon. My dad told it to me. Many times. The Grand Canyon was his favorite place in the world to visit. We must have looked at his slides about a hundred times. I thought they were pretty awesome, but he would always laugh and say, "These pale in comparison to the real thing!"

He was right. I could tell by the sliver of the view I saw through the window between Mallory and David Michael.

I stayed in my seat in the middle of the RV. I didn't really want to see the canyon. I'd been hoping it would be raining or snowing or dust-storming or whatever it does in Arizona. Then we'd just drive past and I would flip through a magazine or take a nap. I wouldn't have to look. I wouldn't have to think about my other trip to the canyon. The one that was canceled when my dad died.

Anna and I were nine. We were so excited. Dad had made all the plans. I remember every detail. We were going to stay at the Mather Campground and take a mule ride into the South Rim. I wanted so badly to try hiking to the bottom, the way Dad had always done, but he said no.

"When you're old enough, Abby, we will," he told me. "If you girls love the canyon as much as I do, I promise we'll go there many, many times together."

We didn't even make it one time.

Just before we were to leave on our trip, Dad was killed in a car accident. Just like that, gone. Our lives fell apart, and so did our plans.

Ever since then, I've barely thought about the Grand Canyon. And I hate when others talk about it. It makes me sick inside. It brings back that whole painful time. It reminds me of Dad's dreams, and mine.

Back when Mrs. Brewer said she wanted to

visit the canyon, I almost choked. I honestly considered asking to stay home.

But if I had done that, I'd have to explain why. And I didn't want to. I didn't want to open it all up again. So I did the next best thing. I tried to convince her to go someplace else. That didn't work, either.

Now, as we approached the south rim, I felt dizzy. My breathing was quick, as if I were running uphill. My eyes were watering.

Outside, the canyon was widening. Inside I felt my own canyon, splitting me down the middle.

It never totally goes away. That was what my guidance counselor said. She told me I would adjust. I would go on with a happy, healthy life. But she warned me about "triggers" — words, images, or thoughts that would remind me of Dad and bring it all back.

This trigger was pulled all the way.

My mind felt like a fortress, fighting off an invasion. But it was losing. The scene was spilling over the top, the scene I've relived a million times in my dreams . . . the pale expression on my teacher's face as I returned from lunch . . . the walk to the principal's office, where Grandpa Morris was waiting . . . the news that forever changed my life into a Before and After.

Abby

It was a long time ago, Abby, I told myself. *Lighten up!*

I swallowed. I breathed deeply.

In the driver's seat, Watson squinted as he read a road sign. "'RV sites . . . Mather Campground.'"

The sound of that name hit me. That was where my family would have stayed!

I tried to choke back a sob.

Jessi turned from the window. "Abby? Are you okay?"

"Yup," I lied. "Just allergies."

I kept it inside. I thought about neutral, unemotional things. Math. Parsley. Sofa cushions.

Luckily, Mather was full. So was the other RV site. No vacancies anywhere.

I tried to contain my excitement. "So we can't go?"

"I saw some other sites back up the highway," Mrs. Brewer said.

She was right. Watson pulled into a campground about a mile south.

Mrs. Brewer was beaming. "Oh, Watson, this is s-o-o-o romantic!"

Karen, Andrew, and David Michael thought that was hysterical. They were giggling like crazy.

Mallory was scribbling in a journal. Jessi was already out of the van, dancing for joy in the parking lot.

"You guys go ahead," I said to Mal. "I'b feelig allergic."

Mallory looked dismayed. "You can't stay here alone. Won't the dry air do you good?"

She was right. It was a dumb excuse.

I pictured Dad in my mind. I tried to imagine what he'd say if he were watching me.

He would be pointing toward the canyon. No doubt about that.

I took a deep breath. I had to face this.

We took a shuttle bus to the canyon. It was crowded, but that didn't stop the three Brewer/Thomas kids from jabbering away. By the time we arrived at the south rim, everyone on the bus knew their names, ages, grades, and favorite foods.

My legs were a little weak as we stepped out of the bus. I was having trouble breathing. I was sure an asthma attack was on the way, so I pulled my backpack around front to reach for my inhaler.

When I looked back up, I saw the canyon.

The breath caught in my throat. Not because of asthma, either.

Because of the view.

My dad had been right. It cannot be described. It has to be seen.

Jessi was already taking photos. Watson was panning a camcorder from left to right. Mallory was still writing. I think she'd already filled up a whole spiral notebook of impressions.

"Let's hike down!" David Michael shouted.

"I want to ride the mules!" Karen said.

"I want to go to the bathroom!" Andrew whined.

Mrs. Brewer took him by the hand and headed toward a complex of shops and restaurants. "We'll be right back."

Ahead of us, a sign read KAIBAB TRAIL. It led down into the canyon. Packs of tourists were taking it, some on foot, some on mules.

Was this the trail Dad had wanted to take us on?

Too many people. They were ruining the effect.

I turned to Jessi. "In case you guys need me, I'm going to take a walk that way." I gestured to the right, where the crowd was much thinner.

As I walked along, a squirrel followed me expectantly. "No food," I said with a laugh.

Soon the crowds were well behind me. Their voices faded, and I could hear the wind echoing below. Or maybe it was the Colorado River, all the way at the bottom. It sounded like whispers.

I sat near a low wooden fence and listened. And looked.

Dad had told me that the canyon started as a river. Over time, the current wore away the

rock, deeper and deeper until it formed a canyon. Nowadays the trail to the bottom is eight miles long.

On Dad's first visit here, he tried to race a friend to the bottom. (Dad was *very* competitive.) They went on two different trails. Dad's was much narrower and rockier. Soon he had to rest. But as he sat, looking out over the canyon, he found he couldn't move. It was as if he'd fallen under a spell. The feeling of peace and openness was so strong he forgot about the race. He just sat there for an hour, silently gazing. He'd never felt so happy and alive.

When I was a kid, I could not understand that story. "Losing a race on purpose is crazy," I said.

Now, for the first time, I understood. I knew why he always liked to return here. And why he had been so eager to take me.

Because now I felt the spell, too. And the peace.

That, I knew, was exactly what he had wanted.

Tears were clouding my vision. I missed Dad so much. But in a funny way, I wasn't sad. I felt that he was there with me. Looking out over the canyon, saying nothing.

Just smiling.

"There you are!"

Karen's voice startled me. I turned to see her

running toward me with a huge beach towel. "Look what we got!"

Behind her was Andrew, speeding along with a toy helicopter, and David Michael with a plastic model of a wolf. Bringing up the rear were Watson, Mrs. Brewer, Jessi, and Mallory.

Karen unfolded her towel as she ran, revealing a landscape with the words GRAND CANYON printed in terrycloth. I don't know how she managed not to trip. "Isn't it gigundo?"

I giggled as the kids surrounded me, all chattering at once.

I tried listening to them. But frankly, my mind was elsewhere.

I was thinking of Anna and Mom. And how much we would enjoy a trip here together.

CHAPTER 20

Mary Anne

Saturday

Standing on Powell Street, I felt the earth move. I thought about the 1906 earthquake. Much of the city was destroyed. Then I thought of the earthquake in the 1980's, when the bridge collapsed.

San Francisco's on a major fault line, so people expect quakes here. When you feel

one, you're supposed
to stand in the center
of a doorway.

I ran to a nearby
apartment building
and stood in it's
doorway, hunched over.

Then a cable car went
rumbling by. A cable
car! That was what
I'd felt.

Everyone laughed.
I had to admit, it
was pretty funny.

Anyway, that
explains the photo
Mr. Schafer took,
in case you were
wondering . . . .

Mary Anne

Click!

The flash blinded me for a moment.

"Mary Anne Spier, protected against all harm!" Mr. Schafer intoned, like a pompous TV announcer.

I could hear Kristy, Stacey, Claudia, and Jeff laughing.

Okay, I was stretching the truth in my journal entry. I did not find this funny.

I was cringing. I felt so foolish.

The cable car stopped and everyone scrambled onto it. "Come on, Mary Anne!" Kristy shouted.

I almost didn't go. It would teach them a lesson to lose me.

Then I realized it would teach me more of a lesson. So I climbed on, too.

As the others giggled and chatted, I just looked at the quaint Victorian houses on the steep, hilly streets.

It's hard to remain in a bad mood in San Francisco. The city has so much positive energy. (I guess you have to be positive to live over a fault line and climb those hills every day.) It's gorgeous, too. Go over one hill and you see a blue bay, spanned by the stunning, orange-red Golden Gate Bridge. Go over another hill and you're in the middle of Chinatown. Another, and you're among glittery theaters and clubs.

We'd only been in San Francisco for a few hours, and I was already in love with it. Mr. Schafer had splurged and rented us rooms at a hotel — one for him and Jeff, and two for the rest of us. We'd checked in and taken a whirlwind tour of the city, and now we were heading back to the hotel garage.

Our next stop? Candlestick Park, home of the San Francisco baseball team.

"Mary Anne, are you having a good time?"

Mr. Schafer's voice startled me. He had moved from the side of the cable car where my friends were. Now he was standing next to me.

"Sure," I replied.

"Good," he said with a smile. "I hope you don't mind my asking. You've been so quiet."

I shrugged. "I just . . . am. That's me."

"I thought maybe you were offended by that photo I took of you under the doorway. You looked uncomfortable."

I did not know what to say. I felt uncomfortable now, too. I'd been feeling uncomfortable since the trip started.

I had wanted to say something to him since

we left the East Coast, but I couldn't. I didn't want to seem ungrateful. He'd worked hard. He'd taken us across the country. He'd been very nice and good-natured and patient. And except for what happened in the badlands, he'd been a good driver.

But so many of his comments were flashing through my mind. Little things. The jokes about my dad. The teasing. The way he made me feel as if I had to defend my family against his.

It didn't seem fair. Why should I have to take that? Just because he's a grown-up? I know if Dawn had been in my shoes, she wouldn't have taken it. She would have said something. Not in a bratty way, but in a direct and honest one. That's the way she is.

But I'd felt funny about talking back to him. He's not even my stepdad. He's just the dad of my stepsister. Is there a name for that? "Dad once removed" or something?

Now he was gazing out from the cable car, smiling in a friendly way. I had to admit, it was nice of him to ask me if I was having a good time. Suddenly he seemed less intimidating.

Maybe he wasn't technically related, but at least he cared.

And if he cared, he'd listen.

"Actually, Mr. Schafer, you're right," I said.

"Right?"

"About the picture. I thought you were making fun of me."

Mr. Schafer nodded. "I figured something was wrong. I'm awfully sorry, Mary Anne. I didn't mean to hurt your feelings."

"Can I ask you a question, Mr. Schafer?"

"Sure."

"I don't mean to sound ungrateful. I've really enjoyed the trip and all . . ."

Mr. Schafer grinned. "That's not a question."

"I know! I mean, I was about to —"

"Gotcha," Mr. Schafer said with a laugh.

A joke. He was turning my feelings into a joke again.

"Maybe it's me, Mr. Schafer," I said. "Maybe I'm too sensitive. But sometimes your humor makes me feel . . . I don't know, awkward. Like that joke you just made. And the jokes about my dad and my family, too. I know you mean well, and I'm not saying you're a bad person. I just . . ."

What was I saying? Mr. Schafer was looking at me as if I were speaking Ancient Greek.

I absolutely *hate* confrontations. I felt tears welling up.

"I'm just . . . blabbering," I murmured. "I'm tired, I guess."

"No, you're right, Mary Anne," Mr. Schafer said softly. "I do have a big mouth. Always have. I've lost a friend or two because of it. You must have felt pretty awful there in the RV. I just wish you'd told me sooner."

"With everyone around?" I asked.

"Good point." He puffed out his cheek and exhaled. "Sorry, Mary Anne. I'll think before I open my big mouth. Hey, even grown-ups aren't perfect."

"I know."

"Close. Very close. But not perfect."

He grinned.

This time, I grinned back.

Boy, what a difference.

I have never felt so good sitting in a pro baseball stadium. Mr. Schafer had been especially nice to me all the way to Candlestick Park.

Not only that, but the San Francisco Giants were winning — and I was actually enjoying the game!

I cheered for a home run. I jumped up to do three waves with the crowd. I even enjoyed a watery hot dog and half-melted ice-cream bar.

By the middle of the seventh inning, the San Francisco Giants were ahead, 9–3.

"And now, ladies and gentlemen, it's seventh-inning stretch time!" the announcer blared.

We all stood up. Mr. Schafer and Jeff took orders and scurried off to the concession stand.

The stadium organist started playing the "Mexican Hat Dance," and we clapped along. Then Kristy and I turned to each other and clapped hands with each other.

The video screen on the scoreboard showed live views of the audience. A dad bouncing his baby to the music. A barbershop quartet, complete with striped suits and straw hats, singing away. An old couple, dancing. Someone in a big chicken costume.

I laughed out loud at that one.

Then the image changed again, and I stopped laughing.

I stopped breathing for a moment, too.

A smiling, handsome man was waving to the camera. He was wearing a bright red shirt. Beside him was a smiling, pretty woman. She was totally unfamiliar.

But he wasn't.

I knew his face. I had seen it every day when I was growing up. It was a little older and grayer. And a touch thinner.

But even now, even with those changes, I could not mistake him.

The image changed, and I turned to Kristy.

Her hands were frozen in midclap. Her face was chalk white.

"Kristy," I said, "was that —?"

Kristy didn't say another word. She didn't need to.

I knew from her expression that I'd been right.

I did know the face.

It was her dad's.

CHAPTER 21

Jessi

Saturday

We made it! We are on the West Coast!

Well, not on it, actually. Inland a few miles. In Balboa Park, at the San Diego Zoo. Hoping the mama panda has given birth.

Andrew is beside himself with excitement.

He's crossed the whole country for this moment.

Actually, I'm pretty excited too. Oh, well, we're about to go in. The next time I write, I hope I have news about

Jessi

"Jessica. Right?"

I was about to finish my journal entry. The words I was going to write were *a baby panda.*

But I didn't get to finish. The sound of Liz Hoyer's voice made me nearly drop my pencil.

I turned and smiled. Liz was bouncing toward me, clutching an armful of brochures. Her grandparents were right behind her, waving.

Yes, Liz Hoyer. Did I ever think I'd see *her* again? Not in a million years. Definitely not at the San Diego Zoo.

Honestly, I was convinced she must have been following us.

"Hi," I called out.

"I don't believe this," Abby murmured.

"What is she doing here?" Karen asked.

"We-e-ell," Watson said, "Mr. and Mrs. Hoyer! Felicitas! How wonderful to see you! Won't you join us?"

Gulp. *Join us?*

"No!" Andrew blurted out.

"Do we have to?" David Michael whined.

"Shhh," Mrs. Brewer said.

The Hoyers didn't seem to have heard the rude remarks. Liz was whispering something to her grandfather as he approached.

"We'd love to!" Mr. Hoyer replied.

I wanted to slink away.

But I smiled. I was going to be a good sport. It was a beautiful day, and nothing was going to spoil my trip to the zoo.

Liz looked grumpy.

"We're going to see the mommy panda have a baby," Andrew informed her.

Liz rolled her eyes. "She is not going to deliver her cub in captivity. The zoo officials returned the pandas to their native habitat."

"What's a havitack?" Andrew asked Mrs. Brewer.

Mrs. Brewer knelt beside him and began translating Liz's remarks.

David Michael looked warily at Liz. "How do you know they sent the pandas back?"

"I can read," Liz declared.

"So can I," David Michael replied.

"So can *I*," added Andrew (which is true).

Liz handed the boys a brochure. "Here, then."

"Well! Lovely day, isn't it?" Mr. Hoyer said.

"Super," Watson replied.

"THEY TOOK THEM TO CHINA?" Andrew screamed.

"They had to," Liz said. "It is too risky to attempt a panda birth outside of —"

"I DON'T CARE! IT'S NOT FAIR!"

Mrs. Brewer was buying our tickets now. As we walked through the entrance, Watson scooped up Andrew, who was sobbing.

211

Jessi

Abby was giving Liz a fierce Look.

I don't think Liz noticed. She was whispering to her grandparents again, and they were both frowning at her.

"Be nice," I heard Mrs. Hoyer say.

Right. That was sort of like asking an egg to grow hair.

We headed for a loading area marked Kangaroo Bus Tours. Liz walked along with us.

"Did you know that the San Diego Zoo has four thousand animals?" she asked.

"I read that," David Michael replied.

"Eight hundred species, too," Liz continued. "And three point three million visitors come each year. Did you know *that*?"

David Michael had taken the brochure from Andrew and was quickly leafing through it. "Uh . . ."

"After this," Liz rambled on, "my grandparents are taking me to the San Diego Wild Animal Park, which is thirty miles north of here."

"Great," I said.

"It's twenty-two times bigger than this zoo."

"Uh-huh," said Mallory.

We boarded the bus. Liz kept talking.

Our tour guide started narrating. So did Liz.

Mr. Hoyer seemed to find this amusing. Mrs. Hoyer gently tapped Liz on the wrist and said, "So bright for her age."

We were dying.

We stepped off the bus at the Children's Zoo. Andrew wriggled out of Watson's arms to pet a potbellied pig. We watched some zoo attendants feeding baby animals who had been rejected by their mothers.

"Weird," Liz remarked. "Why would parents do such a thing?"

When she was out of earshot, Abby whispered, "Maybe the same reason her parents left her with her grandparents."

That was mean. But I laughed.

The bus took us to the pygmy chimp exhibit, where these weird little monkeys chased after each other at super speed. We watched them somersault, bop each other over the head, and clap their hands and feet.

One of them ran right up to us and made the silliest, scowling face.

"It's Kristy!" Andrew squealed.

Abby, Mallory, Karen, David Michael, and I cracked up. It did look a little like Kristy in one of her bad moods.

"Kristy?" Liz was paging through her guidebook. "Where did you find that? This book gives some of the animal names, but I don't see that one."

We ignored her.

Andrew was jumping up and down, imitating the monkeys. It was a relief to see him happy again. No more clinging to Watson, no more complaining about the panda.

He sure had enough to see. At the Tiger River exhibit, we spotted a tiger with milky white skin and a "fishing cat," which has webbed feet and dives for its dinner.

My personal favorite was Hippo Beach. We slipped behind a Plexiglas barrier to watch hippopotamuses dance in their underwater tank. Yes, dance. That is the only word to describe what they were doing.

"She just did a *piqué* turn!" I exclaimed.

"A what?" Abby asked.

"And a *tour jeté!*"

The kids were howling. "We should give them hippo tutus!" Karen said.

"Toe shoes!" David Michael added.

"Hippos do not have toes," Liz informed him.

We saw sea lions and gorillas and naked mole rats. We were hugged by actors in animal suits. We must have watched the koalas for half an hour.

I think the kids liked the polar bear exhibit the best. We could see them swim, too, like the hippos.

Unlike the hippos, though, they had visitors.

On a wooded hill, behind the polar bear pool, stood seven reindeer.

"Rudolph!" screamed Andrew.

"No, they have black noses," David Michael said. "It's Dasher and Basher and Comic and Glickson —"

"Dasher and *Dancer* and *Comet* and *Blitzen*," Liz corrected him.

"Whatever," David Michael snapped. "Where's Santa?"

"I think he is hiding in the polar bear suit," Karen said.

Liz sighed. "You still believe in —"

"*Ahhhhhh-chooo!*" sneezed Abby. "Oops, allergies."

She gave me a sly smile.

As we headed for the bus, Liz was whispering to her grandfather again. This time I could hear her.

"Liz, they're very nice children," he said.

"But I don't *like* them!" Liz replied. "They're boring, and they don't know anything!"

What?

She had it backward. *She* was wildly boring. And *we* didn't like *her*! How dare she? I had half a mind to turn around and argue.

"They invited us to tour with them," Mrs. Hoyer said softly. "We couldn't say no."

"If you don't take me to the Wild Animal Park, I'm going to scream until my face turns blue! Then I will pass out and boy, will you be in trouble."

The next thing I knew, Mr. Hoyer was jogging to the bus. Watson and Mrs. Brewer were just about to board.

"Pardon me," Mr. Hoyer said. "My granddaughter is a bit fatigued, and we're going to walk back to the parking lot. It's been lovely to travel with you!"

Zoom. They were out of there. Liz didn't even look back. But just before she turned away, I could see she was smiling.

So were we.

"Oh, darn," Mallory said with a straight face. "I was going to ask her how many species of plant life there are in the zoo."

"How many hairs on a polar bear," I suggested.

"Pimples on a hippo's belly," Abby said.

"Next stop, the special panda exhibit!" the tour guide announced.

"But they're in China!" David Michael blurted out.

"They're not leaving until the end of the week," the guide said with a smile. "Passport problems."

I thought Andrew would burst with joy. He

didn't stop squealing until we arrived at the exhibit.

What were the pandas like? Adorable. They looked as if they were smiling at us as they chewed happily on bamboo sticks. They were messy, too — letting thin bamboo shards fall all over their round white bellies.

Andrew shook his head and sighed. "If they're going to China," he said, "someone should teach them not to eat their chopsticks."

Kristy

Saturday

The Brewers won.

I think.

I don't remember the score.
I'll find it in tomorrow's
paper.

I don't remember much of
anything. Except what happened
during the seventh-inning
stretch. And I still can't believe
that....

"Are you sure it was him?" Stacey whispered.

"Almost positive," I replied.

I racked my brain, trying to think of the postmark from Dad's last letter. "Sausalito!" I said finally. "Is that near here?"

"That's just over the Golden Gate Bridge," Dawn said. "Is that where he's living?"

"I think so."

"Then this is his home team!" Claudia blurted out.

"Duh," I said.

"Let's find him!" Mary Anne exclaimed.

"How?" asked Stacey. "There are fifty billion people here!"

"How many more innings are left?" Claudia asked.

"I think two and a half," Stacey replied.

"Perfect! They take forever. We have plenty of time." Claudia sprang out of her seat.

"No!" I said.

"*No?*" Claudia repeated.

"Why not?" Dawn asked.

I sat back in my seat, looking out over the ocean of people. I was in a daze.

Dad was somewhere in there. We were in the same stadium.

I remembered a secret birthday wish I'd

made when I turned six: I'd wished that Dad and I would visit all the ballparks together. I'd thought we had plenty of time, a whole lifetime.

We ended up only making it to two: Yankee Stadium and Shea Stadium in New York. Since then, we'd been batting zero. Oh for seven years.

I never thought we'd actually add another one to the list. This was some strange way to do it.

"I don't know if I want to see him," I murmured.

"He's your dad!" Dawn insisted.

"Was," I said. "He left us, Dawn. Worse. He erased us. I mean, I used to write him all the time. I sent him artwork, told him about my ball games, even sent him a tooth I lost. I asked questions, too. Tons of them. Why did you leave, how are doing, did you find a new job, what's the best way to guard against a sacrifice bunt, blah blah blah. I expected him to answer at least *some.* What did I get in return? Three postcards. Hi-how-are-you-be-a-good-girl-love-Dad. And that sneak visit of his — I had to lie to everybody and almost lose all my friends because he wanted to stay hidden. Then he just ditched me again! So now what? If I do see him, what am I supposed to say?"

"Kristy," Mary Anne said, "you have to look for him. You know that. If you don't do it, you'll always regret it."

I felt as if a racketball had leaped up from my stomach and lodged itself in my throat. I knew I was going to cry, and I just hate that.

Leave it to Mary Anne.

She is always right.

I swallowed and stood up. "Okay. Let's go."

We barged up the aisle. Mr. Schafer and Jeff were already heading back with cardboard trays full of food.

"No need to go, we have enough for —" Mr. Schafer began.

"Be right back!" Claudia shouted.

We whizzed into the corridor.

"How are we going to do this?" Mary Anne asked. "He could be anywhere!"

"He likes to sit on the first-base side," I replied. "You can see the batters better from there because most of them are right-handed. Let's start at the top level and work our way down."

I sprinted up the ramp. My legs thumped the cement. People lurched out of the way.

Thinner. Dad had looked thinner. And his beard was gone. He'd had one the last time I'd seen him.

Maybe he was sick. Maybe he was on a health food diet. Maybe his girlfriend was a nutritionist.

If that was his girlfriend.

Maybe it was his wife.

My heart was pounding. My throat felt like a woolen sock.

We emerged in the upper deck. The stands were pretty sparse.

"This can't be it," I said. "He was in a crowded area."

At each level, we split up, running down the aisles, scanning the crowd. No luck.

When we reached the box seats, just behind the dugout, a uniformed guard stopped us. "Tickets?"

"We're sitting someplace else," I blurted out. "But we have to find my dad!"

"All of you?" he asked.

"You don't understand!" I said. "We came all the way from Connecticut. And I know he's here. He was on the scoreboard —"

"He's a player?"

"*No!* He's divorced! I mean, I haven't seen him in a long time, and then I saw his face when the cameras panned the audience, and I don't know exactly where he's sitting, so even if you let me go down, I don't even know if we'll find him, but please please *please* let us look!"

The man pulled out a cell phone. "I'll call the press box. They can page him for you."

That was when I saw the flash of reddish-brown hair. And the little V-shaped grin. And the bright red shirt.

Just above the dugout. Right behind the first-base line.

"DA-A-A-A-A-AD!" I screamed.

He looked up. The V turned into an O.

Then I saw him mouth, "Kristy?"

I bolted past the guard. I nearly fell down the stairs. Dad was edging toward the aisle, stepping over people's legs.

"Dad, it's me!"

I stopped. He stopped. We were both in the aisle now. I was standing one step above him.

I didn't know what to do. Hug him? Scream at him? Jump into his arms? Stomp away? My mind was a tangle.

His eyes were watery.

"Hi, pal," he said.

At the sound of his voice, I had to catch my breath. I remembered the last time I'd heard that voice in my house, when I was little. I remembered the words it had used. Words that traveled through the walls. Words that made Mom cry and made me pull my pillow around my ears.

"Hi," I replied.

"What are you doing here?" he asked. "How did you find me?"

"I, uh, saw you on the scoreboard. I'm here on vacation . . . with my friends."

Mary Anne, Stacey, Dawn, and Claudia were around me now. I could hear Mary Anne sniffling.

He looked up. "Hi, Mary Anne. And these are . . . ?"

"Claudia," said Claudia.

"Right. Kishi. Wow."

Dawn smiled. "I'm Dawn Schafer."

"I'm Stacey McGill," Stacey added.

"Hi. Well. I . . . don't know what to say. Would you like to sit down?"

"Taking the field in the bottom of the seventh . . ." boomed the announcer, *"the Pittsbuuuurgh Pirates!"*

"We can't," I said. "We have to go back."

"Back? Well, can I buy you a Coke?"

"Aren't you going to ask how Mom is?" The words just flew out. I couldn't stop myself. "Or Charlie or Sam or David Michael?"

"Are they here, too?"

"No. Just me."

Dad let out a low whistle. "I wish I could see them."

"Me, too. You could visit. The Brewers. Remember? McLelland Road."

"Sure. I'd like to." Dad pulled a pen and a slip of paper out of his pocket and scribbled something on it. "Here's my address."

As I took it, I heard a voice from my left. "Patrick?"

It was the woman my dad was with. She was sitting in the middle of the section, giving us a funny look.

"Oh," Dad said. "I'd like to introduce you to my girlfr —"

"First up for the Pirates . . ."

"That's okay," I said quickly. "We have to go. Mr. Schafer will be worrying."

"All right. Well, keep in touch."

"You keep in touch," I replied.

"I will," Dad replied with a smile. "I promise. I'll write."

I managed a smile. Then I waved and turned. This time, I wanted to be the first to leave.

And I did not want Dad to see me crying.

CHAPTER 23

Dawn

Sunday

Party time in Palo City! What a great surprise. Well, sort of. Actually, we arrived early. Carol and Mrs. Bruen were still setting up. Kristy started bossing everyone around, so we were done by the time the South

RV pulled in. When my We ♥ Kids Club friends arrived, it was a total screamfest. Jeff says he's lost hearing in one ear.

Now Abby's lip-synching to an Elvis tape. Sunny's dancing with David Michael, Mrs. Bruen with Watson, Mrs. Brewer with Jill. Maggie's chasing Jeff, who'd rather die than dance. Claudia and Stacey are taking apart this ugly frame from a painting Claudia bought. Jessi and Mary Anne are in deep conversation, something about Mississippi. Kristy's giving Mallory an inning-by-inning account of her trip. Andrew's telling Mr. and Mrs. Winslow something about twisters and pillows in the bathtub. Dad is outside with Mr. Choi inspecting the RV.

It feels great to be back home.

Everything is perfect. Except for one thing. Someone brought COLD CUTS as a house gift....

"Processed dead pig slabs!" I exclaimed.

"Sssshhh," said my stepmother, Carol. "Mr. Brewer stopped at the deli on the way. Watson wanted to treat us to lunch. He didn't realize we were having a party."

I transferred the cold cuts to the back of the table. "I can't believe you kept all this a secret."

Dad and Mr. Choi were heading my way, plates in hand. "She did," Dad said. "All those times I called her from the road — not a word."

Carol smiled. "Mrs. Bruen was standing next to me with a broomstick."

Mrs. Bruen is our housekeeper. She was dancing right next to us. "True!" she yelled.

Dad and Mr. Choi were piling up their plates with vegetables, pita bread, and hummus.

"Well, we just inspected the RV," Dad informed us.

"Your father's a good driver," said Mr. Choi.

"We won't tell him about South Dakota, will we?" Dad muttered under his breath.

Mr. Choi didn't hear. He was looking at Claudia and Stacey. They'd finally managed to take the backing off the frame.

"Interesting sketch," he said. "Where'd you find it?"

"Down the street from the Wall Drug Store," Claudia replied. "In South Dakota."

"Mr. Choi is an art dealer," Dad reminded us.

Claudia took out the sketch and handed it to him. "I just liked it."

"Not bad." Mr. Choi held it up to the light. "Another promising art student who wants to be Georgia O'Keeffe."

Claudia and Stacey were staring at the back of the sketch. Their faces went slack.

"M-May I have that?" Claudia asked.

As Mr. Choi handed it to her, she turned it around.

"Oh my lord . . ." Stacey murmured.

Dad, Carol, Mr. Choi, and I gathered around to look.

On the back of the painting, in charcoal pencil, was the artist's signature.

Georgia O'Keeffe.

Mr. Choi looked stunned. "Do you know how important this is?"

"I . . . own . . . an authentic Georgia O'Keeffe . . ." Claudia whispered.

"Early work, clearly," Mr. Choi declared. "Perhaps from her student days. A model for later work. Obviously, the signature would have to be authenticated. If it's real, I believe it has some gallery value."

"Gallery . . ." Claudia muttered.

"Five hundred dollars sound good?"

Claudia snapped back to reality. "Five hundred? That much, for a *sketch*?"

Mr. Choi nodded. "A painting would be worth far more."

"Well . . ." Claudia clutched the sketch to her. "I don't know if I want to let it go."

"Claudia, are you crazy?" Stacey said.

"Am I?" Claudia asked.

"Think of the art supplies you could buy with the money," I suggested.

Mr. Choi dug a card out of his pocket and gave it to Claudia. "I understand how you feel. Consider my offer and let me know."

As he walked off, the Elvis tape ended. Everyone was heading for the buffet table now.

"Dawn, I forgot to tell you, Whitney Cater called," said Sunny. "She can't wait to see you."

"Stephie Robertson's mom wants you to baby-sit next Wednesday," Maggie added.

"Hummus!" Jill Henderson exclaimed. "Scrump-diddly-umptious!"

Maggie Blume, Sunny Winslow, and I exchanged a Look. We refrained from giggling.

That's Jill. Thirteen going on eleven. But we love her anyway.

I love Maggie and Sunny, too. Sunny was loading up her plate, her strawberry-blonde hair bobbing as she chatted with Abby. Maggie was examining Claudia's sketch. (Claudia was examining Maggie's hair, which was light green; and her outfit, tight black leather and Spandex; and her pale, pale makeup.)

I love when my bicoastal friends meet.

"Ewww! Lunch meat!"

Jill had found the cold cuts.

Sunny, Maggie, and I cracked up.

Watson was leaning over the table, sniffing. "What's wrong? Aren't they fresh?"

"I think they're fabulous!" Mrs. Bruen said.

Jeff was dipping his finger in the hummus. "Good stuff."

Carol nearly had a cow. "Jeffrey, stop that!"

Jeff ran off, giggling. Carol chased after him. Mrs. Bruen scooped out the finger-contaminated part of the hummus.

My We ♥ Kids friends were in hysterics. So were my BSC friends.

I was going to miss traveling. I was going to miss Stoneybrook.

But I was not sad. Not at all.

I felt home again. Comfortable. Happy.

Cold cuts or not.

EPILOGUE

Dear Ethan,

I'm home! I hope this letter reaches you before you leave Seattle. (Actually, it doesn't matter. I'm sending a copy to you in New York.)

Guess what? I am going to visit my dad in NYC the second weekend in September.

I was going to invite you to his apartment. Then I thought we might meet instead at this café in my dad's neighborhood. Then I found out about this cool place on Thompson Street.

It's called the Corner Coffee Connection...

See ya there!

Stacey

Mr. Joseph Woodward
Zuni Elementary School
Zuni, New Mexico

Dear Mr. Woodward,
   Enclosed is a specially decorated friendship quilt, with 23 messages from my siblings and their SES friends. They loved receiving the notes from your kids.
   They are also dying to have an exchange trip. I promised I'd ask you. So, I'm asking!
   Please let us know.

                                    With gratitude,
                                    Mallory Pike

DEAR MR. ROMNY,
   YOU'RE LETTER WAS HEAR WHEN WE GOT HOME. I'M GLAD EVRYTHING IS BACK TO NORMAL IN LESSTER. MY MOM SAID I HAD TO RITE YOU A LETER TOO.
   THANKS FOR HAVING US OVER! WE HAD A STORM HEAR YESTERDAY. NO CARS BLUE AWAY. NO TREES FELL DOWN. NOBODY WAS KILLD OR CRUSHED.
   IT WAS BORING.
   CAN WE VISIT AGAIN SOON?
   RITE BACK!
   SAY HI TO ISABELLA!
   DAVID MICHAEL THOMAS I

235

Hi, Mom!
   We made it! I'm really really really sorry we had to leave Stoneybrook to go on our trip. You looked kind of sad.
   But DON'T FORGET — I'll be coming back Thanksgiving AND Christmas !!.!!
   Which reminds me. On the attached piece of paper, I wrote a list of things I need. I know its early in the year, but by Desember I'll forget them. And you know I love suprises!
                    You're son,
                    Jeff

Dear Dad,
   Got your postcard. I want to keep in touch, too. I'd love an actual letter, though. Like, maybe a page or two? Good luck on your job interview. Let me know all about it. Then I will tell you everything about my life too. Okay? Good.
                    Love,
                    Kristy
P.S. Are you actually a Giants fan?

Dear Grandma,

Your answering machine message was waiting for us when we returned. What a nice surprise.

It was _my_ pleasure to see you in Bloomington. Thanks so much for coming all the way up to see me!

Thanks also for paying for everyone's lunch at the health food restaurant. I thought you were so polite about the food there, despite everybody's jokes.

Are you serious about wanting Dawn's recipe for tofu-millet fritters with burdock root sauce? I wasn't sure.

If you are, I'll tell Dawn.

Love
MaryAnne

DEAR ELVIS,

I KNOW THAT IS NOT YOUR NAME. BUT YOU DID NOT PUT YOUR REAL NAME ON YOUR BUSINESS CARD. MY SCHOOL IS HAVING A DANCE. IT IS FOR PARENTS. IT WILL RAISE MONEY FOR OUR SCHOOL. THEY NEED A SINGER.

CAN YOU SING LIKE ELVIS? PLEASE WRITE BACK.

YOURS TRULY,
KAREN BREWER

Ms. Annie Pardell
c/o Dalton Plantation
     Museum
Dalton, Mississippi

Dear Ms. Pardell,?
    Remember me?
I enjoyed meeting you at the plantation. I told my grandmother all about my visit. When I mentioned your name, she said, "Pardell? Is she related to Rosalie Pardell in Tupelo?"

238

Are you? Because
if you are, we
may be third
cousins on my
father's side!
Maybe we did
find out something
about our genea-
logy after all.
Sincerely,
Jessica Ramsey

Hi, BSC !!!!!!!!
I'm sitting in the
sun, thinking of you.
I miss you soooo
much. How was your
flight back? And
Claudia, PLEEEEEASE
tell me what you
decided about that
Georgia O'Keeffe sketch.
We're all dying to know!
Love,
Dawn

Dear Mr. Choi,

I have thot alot about our conversasion. I think your offer was very generus. I look at the scetch evry day now because its on my wall. It makes me feel so inspirred. I think Georgia is rubbing off on me.

That feling is very valuble to me. So I am sorry to say that I will not be selling my scetch.

I hope youll understand.

Claudia Kishi

PRIVATE JOURNAL

Dear Dad,
Everything you said about the Grand canyon was true. I wish you'd been there with me. or maybe you were.. It sure felt like it.

You know what Ive been thinking about? A phase I went through

when I was six.
when I couldn't
stop begging you
for gifts. Remember?
I HATED when you
said no. And you'd
tell me, "There are
two kinds of parents:
one kind gives their
kids fish whenever
the kids are hungry.
The other kind
teaches their kids
to fish. And those
kids can eat for a
lifetime."
   I couldn't stand
fish, so I always
thought that story
was dumb. Now
I think I know
what you were
talking about.

   you taught me
a lot. How to get
along with other
kids. How to
compromise and

share, how to use my sense of humor. One thing you didn't teach me, though, was how to deal with grief.

I had to learn to do some fishing myself, Dad. And I discovered something you knew all along.

The Grand Canyon is one big pond.

I'll be going back. And I'll be feasting. I promise.

Thanks, Dad. I miss you.

Love,
Abby

Ann M. Martin

About the Author

ANN MATTHEWS MARTIN was born on August 12, 1955. She grew up in Princeton, NJ, with her parents and her younger sister, Jane.

Although Ann used to be a teacher and then an editor of children's books, she's now a full-time writer. She gets the ideas for her books from many different places. Some are based on personal experiences. Others are based on childhood memories and feelings. Many are written about contemporary problems or events.

All of Ann's characters, even the members of the Baby-sitters Club, are made up. (So is Stoneybrook.) But many of her characters are based on real people she knows, other times she chooses names she likes.

In addition to the Baby-sitters Club books, Ann Martin has written many other books for children. Her favorite is *Ten Kids, No Pets* because she loves big families and she loves animals. Her favorite Baby-sitters Club book is *Kristy's Big Day*. (By the way, Kristy is her favorite baby-sitter!)

Ann M. Martin now lives in New York with her cats, Gussie and Woody. Her hobbies are reading, sewing, and needlework — especially making clothes for children.

THE BABY-SITTERS CLUB®

Collect 'em all!

100 (and more) Reasons to Stay Friends Forever!

More titles... ▶

The Baby-sitters Club titles continued...

❑ MG22872-2	#88	Farewell, Dawn	$3.50
❑ MG22873-0	#89	Kristy and the Dirty Diapers	$3.50
❑ MG22874-9	#90	Welcome to the BSC, Abby	$3.99
❑ MG22875-1	#91	Claudia and the First Thanksgiving	$3.50
❑ MG22876-5	#92	Mallory's Christmas Wish	$3.50
❑ MG22877-3	#93	Mary Anne and the Memory Garden	$3.99
❑ MG22878-1	#94	Stacey McGill, Super Sitter	$3.99
❑ MG22879-X	#95	Kristy + Bart = ?	$3.99
❑ MG22880-3	#96	Abby's Lucky Thirteen	$3.99
❑ MG22881-1	#97	Claudia and the World's Cutest Baby	$3.99
❑ MG22882-X	#98	Dawn and Too Many Sitters	$3.99
❑ MG69205-4	#99	Stacey's Broken Heart	$3.99
❑ MG69206-2	#100	Kristy's Worst Idea	$3.99
❑ MG69207-0	#101	Claudia Kishi, Middle School Dropout	$3.99
❑ MG69208-9	#102	Mary Anne and the Little Princess	$3.99
❑ MG69209-7	#103	Happy Holidays, Jessi	$3.99
❑ MG69210-0	#104	Abby's Twin	$3.99
❑ MG69211-9	#105	Stacey the Math Whiz	$3.99
❑ MG69212-7	#106	Claudia, Queen of the Seventh Grade	$3.99
❑ MG69213-5	#107	Mind Your Own Business, Kristy!	$3.99
❑ MG69214-3	#108	Don't Give Up, Mallory	$3.99
❑ MG69215-1	#109	Mary Anne to the Rescue	$3.99
❑ MG45575-3		Logan's Story Special Edition Readers' Request	$3.25
❑ MG47118-X		Logan Bruno, Boy Baby-sitter Special Edition Readers' Request	$3.50
❑ MG47756-0		Shannon's Story Special Edition	$3.50
❑ MG47686-6		The Baby-sitters Club Guide to Baby-sitting	$3.25
❑ MG47314-X		The Baby-sitters Club Trivia and Puzzle Fun Book	$2.50
❑ MG48400-1		BSC Portrait Collection: Claudia's Book	$3.50
❑ MG22864-1		BSC Portrait Collection: Dawn's Book	$3.50
❑ MG69181-3		BSC Portrait Collection: Kristy's Book	$3.99
❑ MG22865-X		BSC Portrait Collection: Mary Anne's Book	$3.99
❑ MG48399-4		BSC Portrait Collection: Stacey's Book	$3.50
❑ MG92713-2		The Complete Guide to The Baby-sitters Club	$4.95
❑ MG47151-1		The Baby-sitters Club Chain Letter	$14.95
❑ MG48295-5		The Baby-sitters Club Secret Santa	$14.95
❑ MG45074-3		The Baby-sitters Club Notebook	$2.50
❑ MG44783-1		The Baby-sitters Club Postcard Book	$4.95

Available wherever you buy books...or use this order form.

Scholastic Inc., P.O. Box 7502, 2931 E. McCarty Street, Jefferson City, MO 65102

Please send me the books I have checked above. I am enclosing $_____
(please add $2.00 to cover shipping and handling). Send check or money order–
no cash or C.O.D.s please.

Name _____ Birthdate _____

Address _____

City _____ State/Zip _____

THE BABY-SITTERS CLUB®

by Ann M. Martin

Collect and read these exciting BSC Super Specials, Mysteries, and Super Mysteries along with your favorite Baby-sitters Club books!

BSC Super Specials

BSC Mysteries

More titles ➡

The Baby-sitters Club books continued...

❑ BAI47050-7	#12 Dawn and the Surfer Ghost	$3.50
❑ BAI47051-5	#13 Mary Anne and the Library Mystery	$3.50
❑ BAI47052-3	#14 Stacey and the Mystery at the Mall	$3.50
❑ BAI47053-1	#15 Kristy and the Vampires	$3.50
❑ BAI47054-X	#16 Claudia and the Clue in the Photograph	$3.99
❑ BAI48232-7	#17 Dawn and the Halloween Mystery	$3.50
❑ BAI48233-5	#18 Stacey and the Mystery at the Empty House	$3.50
❑ BAI48234-3	#19 Kristy and the Missing Fortune	$3.50
❑ BAI48309-9	#20 Mary Anne and the Zoo Mystery	$3.50
❑ BAI48310-2	#21 Claudia and the Recipe for Danger	$3.50
❑ BAI22866-8	#22 Stacey and the Haunted Masquerade	$3.50
❑ BAI22867-6	#23 Abby and the Secret Society	$3.99
❑ BAI22868-4	#24 Mary Anne and the Silent Witness	$3.99
❑ BAI22869-2	#25 Kristy and the Middle School Vandal	$3.99
❑ BAI22870-6	#26 Dawn Schafer, Undercover Baby-sitter	$3.99
❑ BAI69175-9	#27 Claudia and the Lighthouse Ghost	$3.99
❑ BAI69176-7	#28 Abby and the Mystery Baby	$3.99
❑ BAI69177-5	#29 Stacey and the Fashion Victim	$3.99
❑ BAI69178-3	#30 Kristy and the Mystery Train	$3.99

BSC Super Mysteries

❑ BAI48311-0	Baby-sitters' Haunted House Super Mystery #1	$3.99
❑ BAI22871-4	Baby-sitters Beware Super Mystery #2	$3.99
❑ BAI69180-5	Baby-sitters' Fright Night Super Mystery #3	$4.50

Available wherever you buy books...or use this order form.

Scholastic Inc., P.O. Box 7502, 2931 East McCarty Street, Jefferson City, MO 65102-7502

Please send me the books I have checked above. I am enclosing $ _____
(please add $2.00 to cover shipping and handling). Send check or money order
— no cash or C.O.D.s please.

Name_____Birthdate_____

Address _____

City_____State/Zip_____

Please allow four to six weeks for delivery. Offer good in the U.S. only. Sorry, mail orders are not available to residents of Canada. Prices subject to change.

BSCM1196